RESCUED BY AN EARL

THE DUKE'S DAUGHTERS (BOOK 3)

ROSE PEARSON

RESCUED BY AN EARL

PROLOGUE

*J*acintha turned to face him, her heart suddenly pounding wildly in her chest. She did not know what had come over her, feeling her blood almost burning with heat as it raced through her veins.

He had only ever been her friend, an acquaintance of the family. She had known him for some time and had never experienced anything like this before. Had he always been this handsome? Had his lazy smile always made her breath catch?

Of their own accord, her hands touched his shoulders and, as they did so, she caught the same surprise in his own eyes. He had not been expecting this, just as she had not. They were both standing together, wrapped in breathtaking astonishment, as if discovering each other for the very first time.

His hands wrapped lightly around her waist, his fingers seeming to burn a hole through her dress and onto her skin. Jacintha could feel a flush rising up from her very core, her cheeks burning with a sudden, fierce heat.

The wind blew lightly around them, tugging gently at

his hair. He was moving closer now, just a fraction, until their bodies were almost fully pressed together. She could not move, could not think, utterly overcome by what she was feeling.

Jacintha had never been in love before, nor felt any kind of particular affection for anyone and yet, standing in the gardens of her home in the arms of a young man she called a friend, she wondered if this was what love felt like. She was so caught up with all that she felt that her very thoughts were in disarray. There was no concern over impropriety, no worry about what her sisters might think should they catch her in such a situation. All she saw was him.

His head lowered and, instinctively, Jacintha closed her eyes. A strong desire filled her, forcing her to tilt her head back just a little, her slippered feet pushing her upwards towards him.

"Jacintha? Where are you?"

He sprang back, his hands torn from her waist, her fingers losing their grip around his neck. Clearing his throat, he gave her a half smile, looking rather abashed, as one of Jacintha's sisters called her name again.

The moment was gone. Whatever might have occurred was gone, blown to the wind by the presence of another. Jacintha tried to calm her frantically beating heart, following him through the gardens towards the rest of her sisters. He was already laughing and smiling but she could not be so flippant. The enormity of what had *almost* passed between them still settled on her. She could not see him the same way any longer. Not now. Not when he had almost kissed her, not when they had almost started down an entirely new path together.

He looked back at her, his gaze warm. It settled on her for a moment and Jacintha held it, aware of what passed between them. There was almost a hunger there, a desire to rush back into another secluded part of the gardens to see if they could bring it to fruition this time. She knew he was going away, knew that it might be some time before she saw him again, and yet how desperately she wanted to be alone with him, even just for one minute more.

But it was not to be.

As the months and years passed, what had almost occurred continued to linger in Jacintha's memory. What could have happened, had they not been interrupted? And why could she never quite forget that moment in the garden?

CHAPTER ONE

The ball at Almacks was just as much of a crush as Jacintha remembered. The crowd of guests was almost overwhelming, and it was rather difficult to find anyone she knew particularly well, even though she greeted a great many people.

"How we are meant to find suitable gentlemen here, I shall never know," Harmonia murmured, as they made their way to a quieter corner of the room. "I am quite sure I shall forget every gentleman's name on my dance card by the time the dance is through!"

"It is rather busy," Jacintha admitted, worming her way through the crowd of guests. "Ah, here is a quieter spot."

She and Harmonia stood quietly to one side of the room, feeling as though they were able to breathe properly for the first time since entering the ballroom.

"Oh, look!" Harmonia exclaimed. "There is Claudia!"

Claudia came hurrying towards them, her eyes bright with happiness. "How wonderful to see you again!" she exclaimed, pressing each of their hands in turn. "Have you only just returned to town?"

"Yes, only just," Jacintha replied, trying to push all questions about Henry from her mind. "Jessica is here too with Lord Warwick. It was she who found us tickets to Almacks."

"Not that you would have been refused, being the daughter of a Duke," Claudia smiled. "Now, have you heard my news?"

Jacintha nodded. "Yes, we heard from Jessica that your brother is in town."

The smile faded from Claudia's face. "Yes, he is, but that is not the news I was speaking of."

Jacintha flushed, a little embarrassed. "I do apologize."

Claudia waved a hand. "Think nothing of it. It is only to tell you that I have accepted an engagement from one Lord Barker." Her eyes filled with delight, her cheeks dusting pink. "We are to be married before the Season's end."

Harmonia exclaimed in delight and pressed Claudia's hand at once, clearly thrilled for her. "How wonderful!"

"My father is delighted," Claudia said, as Jacintha embraced her. "It takes away some of the shame that my brother brings to us!"

Something caught in Jacintha's throat. "Henry?"

"Who else?" Claudia replied, her expression growing sad. "Father gave him his own small estate as a bequest, since he is now of age, and so he has been spending his time between there and London, although more in London since the Season began."

"We have not yet seen him," Harmonia said, throwing a glance towards Jacintha. "It was Jessica who met him at a recital. She said he was very kind."

Claudia rolled her eyes. "Yes, he plays the part of a respectable gentleman very well but I am sorry to say he has become something of a rogue. Much to my father's disappointment of course, for he expected Henry to be a respectable gentleman." She shrugged and gestured towards the rest of the crowd. "But, as he is of age, he is able to do as he pleases. He is here somewhere, so I am quite sure he will introduce himself to you at some point. However, I feel it only fair to warn you that he is not the gentleman you once knew."

"How very disappointing," Jacintha heard herself say, her heart sinking into her shoes. "Thank you for telling us, Claudia. I do hope that does not detract from your own happiness."

Claudia's smile was immediate. "No, it does not. Lord Barker is quite wonderful, and I am sure he will be everything I have hoped for in a husband. You must look for an invitation to our wedding, for I will be sending them very soon."

"Thank you, we will," Jacintha replied, only for a crowd of gentlemen to approach them – some of whom she knew – and begin to request the pleasure of dancing with her.

Very soon, her dance card was almost full and the first gentleman came to claim her hand for the dance. He was pleasant enough and soon, Jacintha forgot all about Henry. She was much too busy considering each and every gentleman she danced with, wondering whether he might be a suitable match. Trying her best to remember their names, she found herself caught up in all that was going on, glad to see that Harmonia was enjoying herself in much the same way as she.

"You have chosen not to seek Henry out, then?"

Jacintha shook her head as she sat with Harmonia, glad for a few minutes of respite. "I think it best not to."

"I have seen him and only had a brief moment to speak to him," Harmonia replied, softly. "When you went out to dance with the first gentleman on your card, I remained with Claudia and she was able to point him out to me. He came over for a minute or so, not long."

"Oh?"

Harmonia shrugged, her mouth a little sad. "I do not ever remember being particularly close with him, but there did appear to be more of a rakish attitude coming from him. When I first saw him, before he approached, he was talking to three ladies at once, and I am quite sure I saw him wink at one of them, right in front of everyone else. Of course, the lady in question had her fan and simply hid her expression behind it, although the other two ladies were both laughing and simpering." She shook her head, her eyes on Jacintha's. "I do not think he is the man we remember."

Jacintha lifted her chin and set her shoulders, trying not to show any kind of emotion, even though disappointment raced all through her. "Well, then I am glad I chose not to seek him out."

"Claudia tells me that she hoped a certain Lady Leticia Hereford might sort him out. Apparently, they have a close acquaintance, and the lady has shown rather a preference for him."

"Has she?" Jacintha murmured, ignoring the way her heart wrenched for a moment. "Then I hope she succeeds in winning him. After all, it must be rather trying for Claudia and for the Earl."

Harmonia glanced over at her. "You are not particularly upset to find out he is so changed, then?"

Jacintha shook her head, her eyes roving over the dancing couples that twirled around the floor. "No, I think not. There are a great many acquaintances here and many more guests that we have yet to be introduced to, so I will not waste my time trying to find only one singular acquaintance, particularly when he does not display a good character. You know as well as I that rogues and the like are to be avoided, and, if Henry – I mean, Lord Musgrove, has become such a gentleman, then neither of us should have any urgency to reacquaint ourselves with him."

Her sister smiled, evidently a little relieved. "I am glad to hear you say that, Jacintha. I was a little worried."

Jacintha laughed, trying to push away the disappointment she felt in hearing about Henry's behavior. "You need not worry about me, Harmonia. I am quite content, I promise you. Besides, my dance card is very nearly full, and I shall be dancing for the rest of the evening, as I'm sure you will be too."

Harmonia nodded and made to speak, only for two gentlemen to draw near to them both, bowing as they stopped in front of them.

"Lady Harmonia, may I introduce my friend, Lord Slate," the first gentleman said. "And, if you are ready, might I have this dance with you?"

Glancing down at her dance card, Harmonia gave him a bright smile. "Lord Westford, is it not?"

"It is," he replied, beaming at her. "Shall we?"

Feeling a little forgotten, Jacintha watched her sister take Lord Westford's arm and go on out to the dance floor, leaving her behind with Lord Slate.

"That was rather abrupt, was it not?"

Jacintha turned her attention to the man as he bowed again, his brown eyes alight with good humor. She smiled and got to her feet, thinking it rude to remain sitting.

"Please, do not worry yourself. I was simply

commenting on how we have both been forgotten by our friends."

"Sister," Jacintha corrected, smiling. "She is Lady Harmonia, I am Lady Jacintha. Our father is the Duke of Westbrook."

He took her hand and bowed over it, looking rather apologetic. "I know this is a most unusual way of introducing oneself, I do hope you can forgive me. Alexander, Earl of Slate."

"Lord Slate," Jacintha replied at once, with a curtsy of her own. "How very good to meet you. Are you in town for long?"

"For the Season," he declared, with a broad smile as his fair hair flopped over his forehead just a little. "And you?"

"For a few weeks at least," Jacintha replied, carefully. "My father's health is not what it once was but he insisted we come."

Lord Slate nodded. "I quite understand," he replied, as the orchestra began to play. "Now, might I request the pleasure of your company for this dance? Although I will admit to being a little surprised you have not already found yourself a partner!"

Jacintha blushed despite herself, growing rather aware of just how handsome the man was. "It seems you are in luck," she replied, with a warm smile. "I would be glad to dance with you, Lord Slate."

"Capital," he said at once, offering her his arm. "Then shall we go?"

Jacintha stepped out with him and joined a set, seeing Harmonia a little further away. As the music began, she fell into step at once, finding enjoyment in both the dance and in her partner's company. Lord Slate was handsome and clearly from a good family with such a title as he had. Could he be a potential match?

Turning her head, Jacintha froze as she saw none other than Henry dancing across from her, his countenance recognizable in a moment. He did not see her and, as she swiftly turned her gaze back to her partner, Jacintha felt her heart clench just a little, as though recalling all that they had shared – and mourning for what they would no longer have.

That friendship is gone, she told herself, as Lord Slate began to converse with her again. *You must forget it, forget him entirely. What you once had can never be again.*

Turning her attention entirely to Lord Slate, Jacintha continued with the rest of her dance without turning her head to see Henry again. Lord Slate was easy to converse with and danced beautifully, his easy smile and kind eyes delighting her. It seemed easier to forget about Henry when she had such an amiable partner.

"I do hope you will not think me impertinent to ask so soon after our dance has finished," Lord Slate began, as he accompanied her from the dance floor. "But might I peruse your dance card once more? After all, I have only had one dance with you, and I do believe that I am permitted to have two. I should like to take advantage of that fact, should you have a space remaining."

Jacintha felt herself blush, smiling up at him. "I do not find you impertinent in the least, Lord Slate. Indeed, I find you very kind."

His smile broadened, his eyes warm. "Then I shall return you to your sister and her friend, shall I? Perhaps you could all do with some refreshment and then I shall return to sign your card."

Jacintha nodded and greeted Claudia and Harmonia before dipping a quick curtsy to Lord Slate.

The very moment he left, Harmonia and Claudia both began to whisper to her at once, making Jacintha laugh.

"Who is he?" Harmonia asked, her eyes wide as she watched him leave. "He is a very handsome man and clearly you have made something of an impression!"

"Oh, I would not say that," Jacintha replied, with a small smile. "He is kind, yes, but I do not know him particularly well so I think we are being much too hasty in suggesting anything of the sort."

Claudia put her hand on Jacintha's arm. "I know Lord Slate by reputation, Jacintha. He is wealthy, of course, with a good title and excellent family. Certainly an interesting sort of fellow. He would be a rather good match for you I think, Jacintha."

Jacintha paused for a moment before shrugging her shoulders. "I am not certain that wealth and title are enough to make him a good match, Claudia. I would get to know his nature first before I decide on anything else."

Lifting one shoulder, Harmonia sighed. "I suppose you are right to be careful, Jacintha, it is just that he did appear to be very taken with you just now."

"And you think I will miss my chance at happiness if I do not take advantage of such regard?" Jacintha asked, teasingly. "I do not mean to laugh at you, Harmonia, but I do not think that Lord Slate is the *only* gentleman in London who might show a preference for me." As she spoke, her mind flittered back to Henry, who, for some inexplicable reason, remained there for a few moments, as though she wished he might be the kind of gentleman to take notice of her.

"Regardless, I think it would be a good idea to continue

your acquaintance with him for as long as you can," Claudia replied, sounding rather practical. "That man has been in need of a good wife for some time and mayhap you are the one he has been waiting for."

Jacintha shrugged, trying not to give the impression that she was rather pleased with Lord Slate's obvious attention. "I shall certainly keep him in mind," she replied quietly, just as Lord Slate and his companion, the gentleman Harmonia had danced with returned with refreshments. Each of the ladies smiled appreciatively and took the proffered glass, although Jacintha had to force herself to sip it slowly, which was a mite difficult given just how thirsty she was.

Lord Slate turned his attention to her again, making her smile as he found her dance card and placed his name down on the one remaining dance.

"How very relieved I am to get it," he murmured, glancing up at her for a moment as he wrote his name. "I will know in future to come and seek you out the very moment you arrive so that I shall have my pick of dances."

Jacintha felt her cheeks warm. "I shall be sure to look out for you," she replied, before she could stop herself.

He smiled at her, his eyes intense in their gaze. "Marvelous. I do hope I will have the pleasure of your company a great many times over the course of the next few weeks."

"You are too kind, Lord Slate," Jacintha smiled, thinking that the gentleman was quite generous in his compliments – rather powerfully so. However, she did not find his attentions unwelcome, even if he was a little forward. "I am sure we shall meet again very soon."

"I do plan to attend as many social events as I can," he replied, his gaze still fixed on her own. "I shall look forward to them all the more if I know you shall be in attendance!"

They talked for some time, discussing a great many

things and Jacintha found herself growing quite delighted with Lord Slate's company, for he was pleasant and quick-witted, making her laugh very often with his bright remarks.

When it came time for her to dance with another gentleman, the man on her card before Lord Slate, Jacintha found herself rather disappointed to have to leave their conversation, wishing that she might stay a little longer to talk with him. However, she satisfied herself with the knowledge that she would soon be dancing with him again, which would give them more time to speak. He was a very interesting man and Jacintha could not help but agree with Claudia – he did appear to be a rather fascinating man and quite a good match for herself!

*V*iscount Henry Musgrove groaned as his sister, Claudia, sat down at the piano and began her daily practice.

"Not today, my dear sister," he moaned, closing his eyes tightly. "Pray, do stop, I beg you. I shall even *pay* you to stop, such is my agony."

Claudia huffed but, much to his relief took her hands from the keys. "You are in rather a bad mood this afternoon, Henry. Whatever is the matter?"

"I am not in a bad mood," Henry replied, firmly. "My head is aching."

"And that is entirely your fault," Claudia replied, with not an ounce of sympathy. "As you can see, I have no such headache."

"That is because you did not drink nearly as much as I," Henry muttered, leaning forward to put his head in between his hands. "Please, Claudia, no more music for the time being."

Rather irritated, his sister came to sit with him, her face lined with irritation. Henry breathed a word of thanks before leaning back and resting his head on the back of the chair, closing his eyes tightly.

"You did not speak to Jacintha yesterday evening."

His eyes flew open.

"*Lady* Jacintha, I should say," Claudia muttered, with a slight shake of her head. "Not that you are not aware of whom I refer to."

"No, indeed, I am very much aware of Lady Jacintha's presence at the ball last evening," Henry replied, sitting up a little straighter. "I made to speak to her, of course, but – "

"You did not try to speak to her in the least!" Claudia exclaimed, her shrill tones making him wince. "Do not try to lie to me, Henry, I was well aware of your movements last evening – or your lack of them. Why did you not speak to her?"

Henry cleared his throat and gave a slight shake of his head. "I intended to, of course, but I did not know how she would receive me."

"A poor excuse," Claudia muttered, shaking her head. "She asked for you, of course. I told her all about Lady Hereford!"

Groaning, Henry dropped his head into his hands. "Leave off, Claudia!" he said, his voice muffled through his hands. "Lady Hereford and I shall never court, shall never marry. We are not all that well suited, despite what you think."

"I think she is rather pretty and exceptionally well-bred," Claudia replied, with a slight sniff. "She would be good for you, Henry."

He did not answer, wishing Claudia would stop foisting ladies on him. He did not need any of them, and certainly not someone he was not in the least bit attracted to. Lady Hereford was, of course, proper and sensible, but that ignited no spark in him. There was no fire, no sense of attraction between them. That was not what he would be looking for, for he could not even contemplate a marriage without that.

"Regardless, I warned Jacintha away from you," Claudia continued, somewhat airily. "I thought it best she knew your true character before thinking of continuing your acquaintance. That was some years ago now, and she need not continue it further. Not when it could potentially harm her reputation."

For a moment, Henry was struck dumb, aghast at what his sister had done. He watched as she sat there primly, a small smile on her face, as though she had done him some kind of service.

"Claudia, I did not wish her to think ill of me!" he exclaimed, his headache roaring into life as he spoke. "What did you think you were doing?"

She blinked at him, as though astonished. "Why? You don't care what a friend from long ago thinks of you, do you? Given that you are so willing to bring shame and embarrassment to the rest of the family, why would it matter what one acquaintance thinks of you?"

Henry closed his mouth, unable to come up with a significant retort. Claudia, looking quite satisfied with herself, rose from her chair and sighed heavily, her hands on her hips. "Is there ever going to be a time when you change, Henry?" she asked quietly. "Are you ever going to stop all this nonsense and begin to honestly search for a wife? You know how Papa despairs over you."

"Nonsense," Henry blustered, waving away her concerns at once. "They do not care tuppence for my behavior, whether it is good or not. All they seek is the continuation of the family line, the *heir* that I must present."

He sniffed and shook his head, ignoring Claudia's disapproving look. "You need not look at me with such frustration, my dear sister. I am quite sure you can be good enough for the both of us, especially given that you are to be wed very soon. Surely that will take mama and Papa's attention away from me for a time!"

For a long time, Claudia simply studied him, her face rather despondent. She did not criticize him nor complain but, eventually, she simply dropped her hands to her sides and began to walk away from him.

"I do not think you know the damage you are doing, even to yourself," she said, softly, looking over her shoulder. "This is not the man you once were, Henry. I am glad I did not introduce Jacintha to you. She would have been even more disappointed had she met you in person."

Closing the door behind her, Claudia quit the room and left Henry entirely alone. He rolled his eyes and sat back in his chair, trying not to let what his sister had said move its way into his heart. He rather enjoyed this life of doing exactly what he pleased. It felt like freedom, given that he had spent a great number of years doing exactly what his father had told him. It had not been unpleasant, simply a lot of hard work, but ever since he had come of age, he had delighted in doing exactly what he wanted instead of what his father wanted. Of course, that had brought his Papa some angst, but Henry had taught himself not to care. His life was already mapped out, a life filled with responsibilities and duties to the title, so why should he not enjoy himself for a few years before that happened?

Throwing himself up from his chair, Henry began to pace up and down the drawing room, finding it harder and harder to battle the thoughts that came his way. He tried to tell himself that he did not care that Jacintha had been disappointed by the news that he was something of a rogue, tried to ignore the hurt that stabbed at his chest, but it soon became overpowering.

Hurrying from the room, he strode to the stables and, within a few minutes, was riding in the confines of Hyde Park. It was early enough that the fashionable lot was not yet out, which gave him very few acquaintances to greet. He appreciated that, his concentration entirely on galloping.

Pulling the horse up, he began to trot across the grass, relieved to discover that his headache had finally gone. Perhaps a ride in the fresh afternoon air was the key to ridding him of it, in which case he would do it much more often.

The park was beautiful, touched by the loveliness of summer. The trees and shrubs practically glowed green, the flowers bringing scents to his nose.

It reminded him of the day he had been with Jacintha in the gardens.

A loud groan escaped his mouth as Henry dropped his head, frustrated with himself. He had not intended to think of her again but it seemed impossible for him to forget her. When he had first seen her last evening, it had taken two glances for him to realize that it was she, his mouth falling open before he had managed to snap it shut. She was more beautiful than he remembered, her blue eyes alighting on him for just a moment before she had turned her attention away again. Her rich brown hair had been swept up with pearls and other gems glistening all through it, matching the shimmering of her cream gown. He had hardly been able to take his eyes from her, finding himself almost in a trance as he watched her. The conversation he had been having had come to an abrupt halt, the music of the orchestra fading as he watched her. Her movements were graceful and fluid, carrying herself with an almost regal air as she danced. He had found himself deeply jealous of the gentleman who partnered her, wishing it were he who stood in that man's place.

Why he had not gone to introduce himself, he did not know. Was it because he had grown a little embarrassed by his behavior, quite astonished to realize just how deeply he had been affected by her presence? Was it because she had turned away from him, had not so much as smiled at him? Had he been afraid of what she would say? After all, he had found himself greeting Lady Harmonia with very little qualms, although he had found her assessing gaze a little discomfiting.

"I *was* rude," he muttered to himself, hating the fact that his sister was quite right in that regard. He could not expect her to come and speak to him, for it was his duty to do so. He should have gone to speak to her as soon as he could, for having greeted her sister, it was only right that he should greet Lady Jacintha as well, especially given that they had been the closest of friends.

More than that.

Closing his eyes for a moment, Henry lifted his head and tipped his face towards the sky, choosing to deliberately remember that moment from all those years ago. He had held her in his arms, and it had just been the two of them in the gardens, with no-one nearby to interrupt. For whatever reason, he had been unable to take his gaze from hers, been quite unable to remove his hands from her waist. She had looked up at him with astonishment in her eyes, her cheeks dusting with color, her mouth parted just a little.

If only he had been quicker! Had he not hesitated, then he would have been able to kiss her long before her sister called her. Would things be different then? Would his life have taken a different path?

Or, inasmuch as he was a rake, was it simply the desire to kiss her that overwhelmed him? Did he simply wish to know what her lips felt like against his, whether or not he could make her catch her breath? A rush of heat climbed his neck, a feeling of shame creeping into his heart. He could not treat Jacintha that way. He was not as low as all that. Lady Jacintha had been his friend at one time and he ought to, at the very least, treat her with the respect she deserved.

"I shall have to seek her out," he muttered to himself, turning his horse back towards home. "At the next event we both attend together, I shall make sure to greet her almost the very moment she arrives." His heart lifted from the ashes of mortification and embarrassment, making him smile just a little. Lady Jacintha would see that he was not as bad as Claudia had said. He would be gracious and kind and try not to think about that moment from long ago.

As he rode back home, Henry knew that it would be a great deal more difficult than simply ignoring it. He briefly wondered if Lady Jacintha herself still thought about him, still thought about that moment, before shaking his head to disperse his thoughts. She would not be as foolish. He had left her long ago and, more than likely, she had long forgotten about him.

Not quite sure why he was still feeling so melancholy, Henry closed himself in his own private study for the rest of the day, choosing to indulge in his father's best brandy in an effort to remove Lady Jacintha from his thoughts.

Much to his disappointment, it did not work.

CHAPTER THREE

"And so it seems our cousin is to call on us very soon." Jacintha looked up sharply as Harmonia sighed, aware of the letter she held in her hand.

"He wrote to you?"

Harmonia nodded, a rather pained expression on her face. "Yes, he did. This is, in fact, the second letter he has sent me."

Jacintha frowned, growing a little frustrated with her cousin. "I thought you made things very clear to him, Harmonia."

She lifted one shoulder and shook her head. "I thought I did. But, apparently, our cousin is very persistent."

"Used to getting what he wants, most likely," Jacintha replied with a grimace. "You cannot entertain him alone, Harmonia. Fill up your dance card the moment you enter a room, tell him that you are quite caught up in conversation with whichever gentleman it is you are talking to."

"I cannot be rude," Harmonia replied, gently. "Besides, I have never found him as repulsive as the rest of you."

"I do not find him repulsive," Jacintha stated, firmly.

"Rather that he is altogether inappropriate for you, Harmonia. Even though I am to seek a marriage of convenience, that does not mean that I will give up hope for an altogether *suitable* husband. Whether you seek love or not, Luke is not the right kind of husband for you."

Harmonia sighed and rolled her eyes, showing a little more frustration than she had ever really done before. "I am well aware of this, having been told the same by each of my sisters," she declared, looking rather ruffled. "Anyone would think I could not make up my mind on such things myself!"

"I did not mean to upset you," Jacintha said, soothingly. "I just mean to look out for you."

Getting to her feet, Harmonia tried to smile but could not quite hide her irritation. "I appreciate that, Jacintha, but I am quite able to look after myself. Do excuse me. I think I need some time alone."

She made to quit the room, only for the door to open just as she reached it, making her almost bump into the butler who immediately held up his hands in apology.

"Sorry," Harmonia muttered, stepping back. "Has someone come to call?"

"A Lord Slate, my lady," the butler replied, handing her his card. Jacintha got up at once, her stomach swirling with a sudden excitement.

"Lord Slate?" Harmonia repeated, looking over at Jacintha who saw a sudden understanding dawn on her sister's face. "Oh, of course. Do send him in. And a fresh tea tray, if you please."

The butler bowed. "At once."

Jacintha smiled as Harmonia came to sit by her. "Thank you," she murmured, appreciating Harmonia's willingness to stay. "I know you wanted some time on your own."

Harmonia waved a hand, apparently forgetting all about what had been said about Luke. "Think nothing of it."

Jacintha sat up straight as Lord Slate entered, rising carefully and curtsying delicately.

"Lord Slate, how good of you to call," she smiled, as Harmonia murmured a word of welcome.

He bowed and smiled back at her, ever the gentleman. "Lady Harmonia, Lady Jacintha. I know I was not expected, so I do hope you do not mind my company for a few minutes."

"No, of course not," Harmonia replied, before Jacintha could say a word. "Did you enjoy the ball last evening?"

"Very much," he said at once, his eyes turning back to Jacintha. "Mostly because I made some new acquaintances."

Jacintha felt her cheeks warm at his compliment, aware of how Harmonia was smiling. It was as though her sister was more than aware that Jacintha was, at this very moment, feeling butterflies flutter around in her stomach.

"I come with another invitation to yet another ball," Lord Slate continued, interrupted only by the arrival of the tea tray. "I am quite sure that you will be flooded with invitations, but I came with a small hope regardless."

Jacintha leaned forward and began to pour the tea, surprised that her hands trembled just a little. *You want a marriage of convenience, remember?* she told herself, sternly. *Having feelings for the gentleman will only complicate matters.*

Handing him his cup, she lifted one eyebrow and smiled. "What is the invitation for, my lord?"

"Oh, goodness, I quite forgot to give it to you!" he exclaimed, putting down his tea cup on the table and pulling a small envelope out of his breast pocket. "Do forgive me. One of my distant cousins is throwing a ball in a few days' time and I come with an invitation to it."

Jacintha took it from him at once, jumping slightly as their fingers brushed. "Thank you, my lord," she murmured, turning the invitation over and reading it quickly. "I do not think that we have any other engagements that evening."

The delight that jumped into his eyes made her blush all the more, aware of just how pleased he was that she would be able to attend.

"How wonderful," he said at once, as Jacintha held out the invitation for Harmonia to peruse. "I do hope that I shall be able to have you both for at least one dance."

Jacintha smiled back at him. "I shall make sure to have my dance card as empty as possible when we first meet," she replied, as Harmonia cleared her throat. "You are very kind to invite us, Lord Slate."

"It is for much my own benefit as yours," he replied, with a slightly self-conscious smile. "Thank you."

They talked for a short while longer before he rose to take his leave, having stayed for the expected length of time. Jacintha bid him farewell, but could not help but let her eyes linger on him as he walked away, finding him to be a well-mannered and quite good-natured gentleman. In fact, just the kind of gentleman her father would approve of.

"I would say that Lord Slate has something of an affection for you, Jacintha," Harmonia murmured, as the door closed. "More tea?"

Rolling her eyes, Jacintha gave her sister a wry smile and shoved her tea cup towards her. "Yes, please. And I would not say that. After all, we have only met once before."

"And yet he has seen fit to call this very afternoon," Harmonia murmured, adding a splash of milk to her cup.

"And we now have an invitation to a ball, one that we – or you – were specifically invited to."

"He is merely being friendly," Jacintha replied, not wishing to make too great a point of it. "Now, would you be willing to accompany me into town?"

Harmonia laughed aloud, her eyes sparkling. "To get a new gown, mayhap?"

"Not a new gown, no," Jacintha replied, joining in with Harmonia's laughter. "But, mayhap, something like a new ribbon or gloves?"

"Or perhaps a new gown, if something catches your eye," Harmonia continued, with one raised eyebrow. "So that you might catch somebody else's eye."

Jacintha shook her head and got to her feet, trying to ignore the rush of heat in her core. "Do you want to come with me, or not?"

"No, I thank you," Harmonia replied, sitting back in her chair. "I think I shall have that time alone now."

Jacintha did not mind that Harmonia had chosen not to join her, for she had her maid for company. Wandering through the streets of London, she looked in almost every shop window, smiling to herself at the thought of the ball. Harmonia had been right to suggest that she was considering an entirely new gown for the occasion, but now that her sister had come to such a conclusion, Jacintha knew she could not do it. It would only make her interest in Lord Slate a little too obvious. However, a ribbon or a new pair of gloves would do quite nicely and she did have a few days to consider what gown she might wear to the occasion.

"Lady Jacintha!"

Stumbling just a little, Jacintha felt herself caught by

strong hands who righted her almost at once, allow her to steady herself before letting her go.

"I knew our meeting would be an interesting one, but I did not expect you to fall at my feet!"

Jacintha looked up to see none other than Viscount Henry Musgrove looking down at her, the charming smile she knew so well plastered across his face.

"Henry," she murmured, brushing her skirts down even though she had not exactly fallen. "How nice to see you."

The smile began to fade from his expression. "I should have made your acquaintance sooner, Jacintha. I do apologize for that. It was rude of me."

"Yes, it was," Jacintha replied, ignoring the fact that she had not particularly wished to speak to him again. "Especially when you chose to greet my sister and not me."

"That was not what I had planned to do," he stammered, his face going almost crimson with embarrassment. "I did wish to greet you but you had a great many admirers. I did not want to interrupt the many conversations you were having. That would have been the height of rudeness."

Jacintha only just managed not to roll her eyes, finding his excuses less than tangible.

"I see," she murmured, looking past him. "Well, it is good to finally have the opportunity to see you again, Henry. I hear you are soon to be engaged. May I wish you every happiness when that event occurs."

He spluttered for a moment, his eyes widening as he stared at her. Jacintha held his gaze steadily, not in the least bit put out. Even if Claudia had been exaggerating, that did not mean that there was not an attachment between Henry and whoever the lady in question was.

"I can assure you there is no such thing between myself and any lady of the *ton*," he cried, making others in the street look around at him. "My sister is, of course, attempting to force me into an engagement I do not wish and is doing her utmost to spread the rumor about so that I might do exactly as she wishes."

"Maybe she is trying to protect your family in the only way she knows how," Jacintha replied, calmly, not holding back from telling Henry exactly what she thought of him. "And from what I saw at the ball last evening, I can quite understand why she is doing so. You are not the man I once knew, are you, Henry?" Ignoring Henry's look of astonishment, she cleared her throat and looked all about her. "Now, do excuse me Henry, I am late already and Harmonia will be wondering where I am. Good day. I do not think we shall have much need to converse again."

She strode away from him, her heart beating so wildly that she could hardly contain herself. Making sure her back was as straight as it could be, she walked quickly away from him, praying he did not come after her. She had been rather surprised to see Henry again, the memory of their last meeting flooding her mind the moment she had looked up at him. He, of course, had been his charming self and she had recalled everything Claudia had said about him. It was best that she make it clear that there could be no deep acquaintance between them, no friendship like there had once been. She did not want to even be associated with him, the disappointment she felt over his change in character cutting deeply into her heart.

As she walked, Jacintha knew she had to forget him and all they had shared. There could be no shared fondness, no secret smiles and private conversations. Her Henry was gone and would remain only as a shadow of her past, never to come into the light again.

CHAPTER FOUR

*B*y the following afternoon, Henry was still rather displeased with the way his first meeting with Lady Jacintha had gone. He had expected her to be even a little bit pleased to see him but her stinging rebuke had hit him hard.

He had not allowed it to get to him, of course, for he had simply gone out to the musical recital he had been expected to attend and had carried on as normal. He had even managed a stolen kiss with the beautiful widow of Lord Tunbridge, who, he had heard, was rather good at sharing her favors. He had drunk too much, laughed too loudly and lost too much money at the card table which, all in all, he called a very successful evening.

However, by the time morning came and Henry had found himself wakening up in Whites instead of in his own bed, something like a hammer seemed to strike him over the head.

He had looked around at the rest of his friends, who were all either still drunk or sound asleep on the floor or sprawled across tables, just as he had been, and suddenly

Jacintha's words would not leave his mind. *You are not the man I once knew.*

Through the filth and dirt of London's streets, he had stumbled home, his legs weak and powerless. He had hated his weakness, hated retching on the side of the road, hated the way he had men lower in status than he mocking him directly. His family was ashamed of him and, finally, Henry began to understand why.

After he had slept for a few hours, Henry had been forced to rise. Being washed, shaved and dressed had done little for his dejected thoughts. Glancing at himself in the mirror, aware that he looked much more like a gentleman than when he had first arrived home, Henry had taken in his sunken, red-rimmed eyes and the paleness of his cheeks and had been forced to turn away from his reflection. The shame he felt was too much to bear.

Now, sitting alone in the drawing room, Henry tried to reflect on what had occurred since he had first laid eyes on Jacintha, trying to work out why her presence had affected his behavior so much. His parents had given up trying to talk to him a long time ago and even Claudia, who still railed at him from time to time, was becoming less vehement in her frustrations. It was as though they considered him a lost cause, that he would continue to behave this way regardless of what they said. He had never cared about them before, so why did he care now? What was it about Lady Jacintha that had forced him to consider his behavior?

Growling aloud, he put his head in his hands, wishing it did not ache so. His father had returned to his country seat earlier that day when Henry had been still abed. He had not even shown his father the courtesy of wakening so as to bid him farewell. He knew that would have cut deeply. His mother and sister were most likely out visiting friends, or with Claudia's betrothed, and Henry knew he was not wanted there either. Why did this bite at him now? Why did he care? Lifting his head for a moment, he let a long sigh escape his lips. It was all because he could not rid himself of the memory of holding Jacintha in his arms. Even after all these years, he had never forgotten her.

"Henry!"

The door flew open, startling him, and much to Henry's surprise, in walked his uncle.

"Uncle," he stammered, managing to get up from the chair and shake his hand. "Whatever are you doing here?"

His father's brother, the Honorable Roderick Larch-mont, was tall, with broad shoulders and kind eyes. He had always made the most of being brothers with an Earl, using his own title and influence to do as much good as he could. Of course, being close with his brother, Roderick, had at times helped him with his business matters, and he had taken Henry under his wing.

"I came to see you," Roderick replied, sitting down after embracing Henry into a tight hug. "It has been too long since I have seen you, Henry."

Henry, still a little stunned by his uncle's presence, sat down quietly and stared at him. "You came to see me?" Something foreboding was in those words and, with a rueful smile, Henry pointed his finger at his uncle. "You mean, my father wrote to you."

Roderick smiled, his eyes still as kind and as wise as Henry remembered them, although his thick brown hair was greying at the temples. "Someone has to try and talk sense into you, Henry, and since it appears you will not listen to your mother, father or sister, they thought it best that I try."

Blowing out a long breath, Henry sat back in his chair

and felt shame cover him like a blanket. "I am not sure I will need too much of a talking to, Uncle."

"Oh?"

Henry shrugged, feeling more than a little embarrassed. "I am aware that my behavior has been a little less than it ought to have been of late."

There was a moment of silence. "Henry," his uncle said, his tone low and words carefully chosen. "Your father is constantly paying off your debts, your mother sees you laughing and trifling with as many young ladies – or widows – as you can. Meanwhile your sister is trying to plan a wedding and does not need to be concerned by her husband-to-be choosing to align himself to a better family!"

"A better family?" Henry scoffed, rolling his eyes. "You need not try to emotionally manipulate me, Uncle. I am aware that I have disappointed Mama and Papa but Claudia and Lord Barker are monstrously happy. They would not allow my ridiculousness to affect their future happiness."

"Are you quite sure about that?"

His uncle's question hit Henry right between the eyes. "You cannot be serious, Uncle!"

"I know that there are questions being raised by his family," came the quiet reply. "They are asking what kind of Earl you will be, whether the connection to your family will be a good and prosperous one."

Henry closed his eyes, a pained expression on his face. He had never once considered that his own sister's happiness would be put in jeopardy by his actions!

"I know this is difficult to hear, but you are not the man you need to be," his uncle said, firmly. "In fact, Henry, you are choosing to be the kind of man you ought *not* to be."

"I didn't think I'd be hurting anyone," Henry muttered,

passing a hand over his eyes. "I just wanted to enjoy my freedom."

"I think you have been enjoying a little too much," his uncle replied, quietly. "So much that you have forgotten the responsibilities that come with being the heir to as esteemed a title as Earl."

There was a long silence. Henry did nothing but sit with his head in his hands, his eyes closed tightly and pain rippling through his mind. He had been enjoying every moment he had of his freedom, thinking that he could do exactly what he liked without consequence, only to discover that everything he did was being watched – and noted.

"I know you do not want to harm your sister's future."

"No, I do not."

"Nor do you want to harm your own," his uncle continued. "Do you really think you will find a suitable wife when the time comes, given your behavior?"

Henry lifted his head, frowning heavily. "Uncle, when the time comes for me to marry, most of the *ton* will have forgotten every single mistake I ever made. I will no longer be the talk of the town. They will have moved onto others by then."

"Do not be so sure," his uncle said, darkly. "You can never tell what your actions will do to your future. An earl is to be responsible and honest, hardworking and attentive to all his duties. Can people look at you and know that you will be that kind of man?"

Henry paused before he answered, remembering all the times he had spent with his father, going over and over accounts and the like. He had been taken to visit the estate's tenants repeatedly, overseeing the repairs to their homes and ensuring the land was being cared for. There were harvests and plantings, horses to look for, shooting to arrange. He had balked at it, glad when he had been given the freedom to live as he wished, never thinking any more about it. And not only had Jacintha spoken to him about his behavior, he now had his uncle doing much the same thing.

"I have been foolish, have I not?" he muttered, shaking his head to himself. "I confess that it is not only you who has spoken to me of this, but another previous acquaintance with whom I have only recently just met again."

His uncle lifted an eyebrow. "And was this acquaintance glad to see you?"

"She might have been, had I been the same man she once knew," Henry admitted, sadly. "Her words were harsh but fair, even though I was unwilling to admit it."

His uncle chuckled, breaking the sudden tension. "A woman is always likely to spark things within the depths of our hearts."

It was on the tip of Henry's tongue to say that he did not have any kind of feeling for Jacintha, that their relationship was not of that ilk, but he found that he could not quite say it. He *did* want to get to know Jacintha again, wanted to show her that he was not the man she had seen when she had first come to town. He could be the man she had once known again, could he not? He would prove it to her, in the hope that she would, at the very least, allow him to be her friend once again. Could he hope for more than that? Did he *want* more than that?

"I have a proposal for you," his uncle said, breaking into Henry's thoughts. "You may reject it outright if you wish, and I will not be offended – but it is just a thought."

"Yes?" Henry asked, looking over at this uncle. "What is it?"

His uncle cleared his throat, looking a little uncomfortable. "I have, for some time, been involved in an operation that attempts to put an end to the smuggling going on around England's shores."

Henry blinked, finding himself astonished once again. "Smuggling?"

His uncle shrugged as though it were commonplace to find a titled gentleman doing such a thing. "I have a small property near the coast, close to the Dover beach. The small town of Ferryway – not that you'll have heard of it. There is a great deal of smuggling going on – the usual goods of liquor, wool and tea - and the operation is only just beginning. We are in need of good, strong men to assist us."

"I see," Henry said, slowly, studying his uncle carefully. "And what would it involve?"

"Patrolling, mostly, with reporting back to the rest of the group about what we have discovered. At times, there might be the need to bear arms or to board a ship. I know you are good at both."

Henry chuckled, aware that his uncle had been the one to teach him to fight. "Yes, that is true I suppose."

"We are a group of all kinds of men," his uncle continued, with a smile. "That means we are not all titled, nor do we all have great fortunes. We work together, as one. There is no snobbery, no arrogance, or the like. You will have to lose such airs and expectations, should you come to join us."

Henry drew in a long breath, aware that this did not exactly sound enticing.

"I know it is a great deal to consider but I believe it will be the making of you," his uncle finished, slowly. "I am here until the week's end. Might you decide by then?"

"Certainly," Henry agreed, aware that he had very few invitations as yet for the following week. "I have a few more engagements this sennight but I should be able to find time to consider your proposal."

His uncle chuckled, shaking his head. "Very good, Henry. I will not press you to decide one way or the other. Only know that I have the very best of intentions for you."

"I do know that, uncle," Henry replied, honestly. "And I thank you for your concern. Even if I do not come with you to Dover, you can be assured that I will take your words with the very greatest severity. Truly."

"Thank you, Henry," his uncle said, quietly. "Think it over. That is all I ask."

CHAPTER FIVE

"*M*ight I have the pleasure of your company?"

Spinning around on her heel, a ready smile on her face, Jacintha made to greet Lord Slate, only to see that it was, in fact, Lord Musgrove. Her smile faded at once, the brightness of her eyes dimming.

"Oh," she mumbled, as he took her dance card from her limp wrist. "Henry. I mean, Lord Musgrove."

He chuckled, patting her hand. "We need not worry too much about titles, Lady Jacintha, not unless you believe there is someone watching. We are old friends, are we not?"

"Yes, of course, but – "

"Then I shall look forward to having your company very soon," he interrupted, smiling broadly at her. "In two dance's time, I believe."

Jacintha struggled to find a response, knowing that she ought to show some kind of gratefulness towards him for his kindness in asking to dance with her, but found she could not even muster a smile. She did not want to dance with Henry, and she had thought she had made that quite clear when she had met him in town two days prior. However, it now seemed that he was quite determined to have her company, which she was not best pleased about.

"Might I sign my name, Lady Jacintha?"

Lord Slate bowed in front of her, only for his smile to slip as he took in her expression.

"Have I upset you in some way?" he asked, looking gravely concerned. "Whatever it is, Lady Jacintha, I beg you to tell me!"

"No, it is not your doing in the least," she replied at once, managing to shake off her frustrations. "It was just that I have already had a gentleman sign my card, and I did not particularly wish to dance with him."

"You have had more than one gentleman seek a dance with you, Lady Jacintha," he chuckled, lifting her dance card. "How glad I am that there are a few spaces left for me!"

Jacintha laughed, glad that he had relieved her tension for the moment. "You know very well that I am looking forward to dancing with you, Lord Slate. You need not seek compliments from me."

"I am only sorry that I shall have to wait a little longer than I had hoped," he replied, with a somewhat melancholy expression. "However, I shall look forward to when I have you all to myself for a time."

Jacintha felt her cheeks burn although, much to her dismay, Henry came to claim her just at the same moment as Lord Slate turned away. She had no other choice but to turn to him and away from Lord Slate, wishing that she had been able to avoid Henry completely somehow.

However, the moment Henry took her in his arms, Jacintha found she could hardly breathe. He had, of course, claimed her for one of the waltzes and she soon found herself spinning around the floor as Henry held her tightly – although at the appropriate distance.

"You dance very well, Jacintha," he murmured, his eyes catching hers.

"Had you not expected me to?" she replied, a little sarcastically, in an attempt to rid herself of the heat rifling through her.

He chuckled. "Goodness, you are determined to dislike me, are you not?" He leaned a little closer, his arms tightening around her just a fraction. "Why? Is it because you cannot forget what *almost* occurred between us?"

Jacintha swallowed hard, unable to keep his gaze any longer. "No, indeed. I have only just now recalled it, when you brought it up. In truth, I am relieved that it did not occur, not when you have turned into a rogue."

"Mayhap I would have never become such a thing had you been by my side," he murmured, his breath whispering across her cheek. "Mayhap you are the one to change me, Jacintha."

She could not answer, her breath coming quick and fast as they danced. She was sure her cheeks were red, desperately hoping that he could not hear the hammering of her heart.

Why was she having this reaction? She had tried to push him away, tried to forget the moment he had almost kissed her all those years ago and yet, the moment he had her in his arms, her senses had begun to swim and she felt as though she were walking on air.

It was all quite disconcerting.

"I am disappointed to have to leave you," Henry murmured, as the dance came to a close. "Our second dance is not until much later. I look forward to having you by my side once more, Jacintha."

She did not respond, wishing she could fan her hot cheeks but knowing that, if she did so, it would only draw attention to her. It was a rather great relief that Lord Slate came to claim her hand soon afterwards, albeit after two other gentlemen for whom she did not particularly care for.

"Lord Slate," she breathed, as he led her to the dance floor. "I am relieved to have you by my side, I must say."

He chuckled. "Someone trod on your foot, did they?"

She laughed, relief rippling all through her. "Not quite, although they were not exactly graceful."

"Then I shall do my best to make up for them all," he replied, his eyes glittering for a moment, the small curve of his lips making her tingle. "You ought to be treated like a precious jewel, my dear Lady Jacintha. Delicately and carefully at all times."

"Does that mean I sparkle beautifully?" she asked, unable to prevent herself from teasing him.

He lifted one eyebrow, his lips curving upwards. "Always," he replied, softly, before the music began to sweep them away.

Jacintha could not get his words from her mind as they danced, forgetting entirely about Henry and the strange feelings he had incited in her. Lord Slate was an impeccable dancer although, much to Jacintha's chagrin, he lacked the passion that Henry had exhibited. He did not bring any of the same emotions to her as Henry had done, nor did she feel any kind of warmth growing in her heart. Even though she cared for Lord Slate and certainly welcomed his attentions, there was no quickening of her heart when she took his hand, no heat climbing up her neck and into her cheeks when he placed his hand delicately on her waist. How strange it was to have such an entirely different experience with a man she knew was more than suitable for her!

But, you do not wish to have any kind of passion between you and your husband, Jacintha. You want a practical, well thought out arrangement. So what does it matter?

"You look as though you have a lot on your mind," Lord Slate said quietly, as he took her elbow to lead her from the dance floor. "Are you not enjoying the evening?"

Jacintha was a little surprised that he led her to a quiet corner of the ballroom instead of back to her sister, but went with him regardless, knowing she had nothing to fear from him. "I am enjoying myself a great deal, Lord Slate. You need not worry about me."

"And yet I find myself quite caught up with you," he replied at once. "My dear Lady Jacintha, you can have no doubt that I am choosing to seek out your company."

A slight anxiety caught her heart, making her fingers tighten as she twined her hands together in front of her. "Lord Slate, we have only known each other for a sennight!"

"And yet I find it more than long enough to be aware of what my heart is feeling," he replied, warmly. "I will not pretend that I do not have every intention of speaking to your father and requesting to court you – but only if you will agree."

Jacintha did not know what to say, finding it rather strange that they were having such a discussion in the midst of a ballroom instead of during an afternoon visit. "I – I am surprised that you would ask me such a thing here, Lord Slate," she stammered, finding that she was rather unsure of her answer. "I mean, this has taken me by surprise."

"How can it?" he exclaimed, reaching for her hand and taking it in his own. "I have come with a personal invitation to a ball and quickly sought you out so that I might have the pleasure of dancing with you. I know our acquaintance has been of short duration but will you not consider me?"

Jacintha hesitated. To agree to be courted meant that she was, in essence, agreeing to a relationship with the man. Most couples who courted in earnest soon became engaged, which meant that she had to be quite sure of Lord Slate.

"I would ask you to give me a little more time to get to know you, Lord Slate," she said slowly, her heart dropping in relief at her answer. "Our acquaintance is a short one and you have only called upon me the once. I do hope that you understand what it is I am saying and I must, of course, let you know how deeply appreciative I am for such a request. That is kindness in itself."

He lifted her hand and, much to Jessica's astonishment, turned her gloved hand palm upwards and pressed his lips to it firmly. It was such an intimate gesture that it made her gasp, going crimson with embarrassment and desperately hoping that no-one had seen him do it.

"I should return to my sister," she whispered, tugging her hand away from him. "And I will need to dance again soon. Thank you, Lord Slate."

She did not wait for him to respond but quickly hurried away, glancing all around her to ensure no-one had seen him do such a thing. Had they noticed, then rumors would start and her reputation might be stained. Why had he done such a thing as that? Was it so that he might do exactly as she feared, in the hope that she would have no other choice but to marry him?

She shook her head to herself, her heart beating frantically in her chest as her worry rose. Much to her relief, there did not appear to be anyone looking at her. She was quite safe.

It was only then that she happened to glance up, recalling that there might be people in the balcony looking down at them. To her horror, she saw none other than

Henry Musgrove looking down at her, his lip curling. He had seen her. He had seen what Lord Slate had done.

"Oh, Henry," she whispered, fear clutching at her heart. Would he tell others of what he had seen, just to spite her for her harsh words? She could not take that risk. There was no other choice but to go to him, to speak with him and explain what had occurred. Surely he would not do such a thing just to be spiteful? After all, he had done much worse than she ever had, and a small kiss to the palm of her hand was nothing!

Gathering her skirts, Jacintha made her way quickly through the crowd, heading towards the staircase so that she might make her way up to the balcony in order to speak to Henry. She had to be sure of what he had seen – and to make sure that he would not speak of it to anyone.

CHAPTER SIX

*H*enry had very much enjoyed his dance with Jacintha. The moment he had taken her in his arms, the past had come back to hit him full force, and he had been forced to draw in a sharp breath. She was even more beautiful than she had been back then, her nearness having such a great effect on him that he couldn't find the words to explain all that he was feeling.

He had laughed and smiled and teased her, but she had not been so ready with her smiles. Her guard was still up, protecting her from him – but he had been bolstered by the fact that she had blushed deeply when he'd pulled her just a little closer.

Maybe she *did* remember their moment in the gardens, even though she stated she had pushed it out of her thoughts. Jacintha had never been able to lie particularly well, for she had always looked away from the person she had been speaking to as the words flew from her tongue, and, as they had been dancing, her gaze had shifted to somewhere past his left shoulder. Had she been hiding the truth from him? Did she remember more than she wanted to admit?

That would be a delicious truth.

Leaning forward, Henry leaned on the balcony rail and looked out at the swirling dancers. He was not at all pleased to see Jacintha dancing with Lord Slate for he had noticed that Lord Slate seemed particularly interested in the lady. Not that Jacintha could not dance with whomever she chose, but Henry would prefer that she had no specific acquaintances as yet. It meant that he would have more time to prove to her he was not the man she had first seen on her arrival in London.

Frowning to himself, he thought about all his uncle had suggested. To go to the Dover coast would be to remove himself far from London town and all its pleasures. He would be changing his evenings of dancing and music to walks on the beach and conversations with the working class. His nose wrinkled.

Snob!

The thought had him wince, guilt washing over him immediately. His uncle, brother to an Earl, was doing a wonderful job for the Crown and clearly did not find it particularly difficult to mix with those of a lower class. In fact, the way he had spoken of them gave Henry the suggestion that his uncle found them worthy of respect. Chewing on his lip, Henry supposed that this was because the working man had to do a great deal of hard labor in order to provide for his family – and here he was thinking that balls and soirees were the light of life! His head dropped for a moment, his chin almost resting on his chest. Where was his compassion for those of lower class than he? Where was his desire to help the poor? When the time came for him to take on the title of earl, he would have tenants to care for. Tenants who would work hard from dawn till dusk, preparing the land for planting and then, much later, harvesting the profits of their labor. And he would remain within his estate, simply focusing on accounts and the like instead of putting his own hand to the till. Did these men not deserve some kind of respect from him?

He drew in a long breath, wondering whether he should accept his uncle's proposal. Mayhap it would be what he needed to improve his own character. It would be a chance to push away his vices and desires, focusing only on doing something profitable for a change. Something of use, something to help others instead of himself.

Lifting his head, Henry sighed and looked out at the dance floor again, realizing that the only reason he had not agreed to his uncle's suggestion was because he did not particularly want to give up London. He liked it here. He liked the balls and soirees and recitals, and all that went with it! It came down to sheer selfishness on his part.

His eyes searched for Jacintha but he could not see her. His gaze narrowed as he continued to look for her, wondering which gentleman had come to claim her now. Finally, after much searching, he found her standing to the side of the ballroom with none other than Lord Slate.

His heart sank as he saw her smile, only for Lord Slate to reach out and take her hand. Henry supposed that the gentleman thought he would not be so easily seen over at this corner of the room, although he personally did not think that to take a distinguished lady such as Jacintha into the corner of a room in such a surreptitious manner was a wise idea.

His mouth dropped open as he witnessed Lord Slate lift Jacintha's hand to his lips, only to turn it over, palm up, and press a kiss there. A kiss to the back of the hand where the lips touched the glove would be surprising in itself but to kiss the palm of the hand spoke of a great intimacy between the two.

His heart roared with pain, his hands whitening on the balcony rail.

Was there something more between Lord Slate and Lady Jacintha? Why had she followed him to the quieter area of the room? Why had she allowed him to do such a thing?

Unable to drag his eyes away from the situation, Henry saw that Jacintha looked almost as astonished as he felt. Her eyes were wide, her mouth slightly ajar. He could not guess what it was she was saying but she was clearly taking her leave of the man. Mayhap she was discomfited by what he had done?

White hot anger shot straight through him, making his entire body stiffen. He could not take his eyes away from her as she walked away from Lord Slate, seeing her look around as though worried someone had seen what Lord Slate had done. He watched Jacintha take in a deep breath, one hand pressed to her heart as though trying to calm the frantic beating that went on deep within her chest.

And then, she looked up at him.

Henry saw the fright in her expression, the worry that creased her brow. And yet, he could not remove the anger and upset from his own features. His brow furrowed, his eyes growing narrow as he watched her, seeing her start towards the staircase.

Apparently, she wanted to speak to him.

His gaze returned to Lord Slate who was, by this point, now talking amicably to some other gentleman. He did not seem in the least bit concerned about what he had done nor if anyone had seen. Was he hoping that someone might have witnessed his inappropriate gesture? If a rumor started, then Jacintha might be forced into matrimony – although whether she was hoping for marriage to Lord Slate, Henry could not say.

"Henry."

Jacintha's words were quiet and he turned around at once, seeing her pale features looking back at him. Her breathing was slightly ragged, as though she had rushed to get to him.

"Henry, that was not what it looked like, I – "

"Why should I care what you and Lord Slate do?" Henry interrupted, rather brusquely. "That is your business, Jacintha."

"Henry," she said again, almost pleading with him. "Henry, I must know that you will not speak to anyone of what you saw."

His lip curled. "And that is the only reason you are come to speak to me, is it?"

She looked at him helplessly, her eyes a little damp. "I – I cannot have this spread about, Henry."

He snorted, unable to contain his frustration. "I see. And you think that a rogue like me enjoys putting rumors about, do you?"

"No, I – "

"As I said before, Jacintha, I do not care what goes on between yourself and Lord Slate. I have much more important things on my mind."

Looking back at her, he saw that she looked even more confused than before, clearly unsure as to why his manner was such an angry one. He did not feel the need to explain, his heart hammering in his chest and his hands curling into fists.

"Lord Slate was much too forward, Henry," he heard

Jacintha say, as he turned away. "I was shocked by his action and I am worried that it will be spread about. I think you are the only one who saw."

"And you think so little of me that you believe I would spread such things about without even considering the impact such a rumor would have on you and your future," Henry retorted, rounding on her. "Goodness, Jacintha, I knew you thought ill of me but I never expected it to be as bad as all that! I think I had best take my leave. Good evening."

He did not wait for her to respond to him but turned around at once and began to walk away, leaving her standing alone on the balcony. The anger he felt pushed at him to hurry away, the hurt of her expectation of his behavior cutting deep.

She truly thought that he was the kind of gentleman who would spread rumors? Who would enjoy sharing gossip – even gossip about a lady he considered his friend? That pained him.

He left the ball, a stale taste in his mouth. This no longer pleased him, no longer gave him the enjoyment he had once derived. He finally saw himself in all his ugliness, finally saw himself as Jacintha saw him. He had to find his true character again, had to rid himself of all the vestiges of the life he had thought he enjoyed. It was time to leave London, time to put this place and all its frivolities behind him. He would return by the end of the Season in the hope that Jacintha was neither married nor betrothed, desperate to show her his true self. Desperate to show her that the man she had once known was still there. He needed to show her that he had never forgotten her, that the feelings he once had still rose in him – but he could not do that when he was considered a rogue and a rascal.

"Uncle," he said, the moment he stepped into the drawing room and found his uncle sitting by the fire. "I have decided."

His uncle Roderick looked up at him in surprise, setting the book he had been reading down on his lap. "Oh? And what have you decided?"

"I want to come with you, if you will still have me," Henry replied, absolutely firm in his decision. "I will leave tomorrow if you so wish."

His uncle got to his feet and held out his hand, shaking Henry's firmly. "Good for you, Henry. We can leave tomorrow if you wish. I promise you, you will return to London a changed man."

"A change for the better," Henry replied, his thoughts still centered on Jacintha. "Thank you, uncle. I am already looking forward to it."

CHAPTER SEVEN

*J*acintha knocked lightly on her father's study
door, hearing voices coming from within. She
waited until she was called to enter, only to see
none other than Lord Slate inside.

She stopped dead, staring at him.

"Jacintha," her father said, warmly. "Lord Slate came to
introduce himself to me only this afternoon." He chuckled
and shook his head. "Of course, I am entirely unaware as to
what my daughters get up to when they are out and about
within society, for I can very rarely find the energy to go to
such things. Thankfully, their older married sister, Jessica,
can chaperone them."

"And a wonderful job she does too," Lord Slate replied,
with a slight bow. Coming towards Jacintha, he bowed
deeply and smiled at her, his eyes bright and alive with
happiness. "Might I call upon you tomorrow, Lady
Jacintha?"

Jacintha could not quite think clearly, her mind working
furiously to make sense of why Lord Slate was in her
father's study.

"Tomorrow, Jacintha?" her father repeated, a little loudly. "With Lord Slate?"

"Y-yes, of course," Jacintha answered, closing her eyes and shaking her head just a little. "I do apologize, Lord Slate. I am just a little tired after last evening."

Lord Slate chuckled and made to reach for her hand but Jacintha quickly put both hands behind her back, clasping them together. She did not want a repeat of what had occurred last evening.

"Then, I shall bid you a good day," Lord Slate continued, after a slightly awkward pause. "Thank you for meeting me, Your Grace. I do hope to see you again."

The Duke nodded and smiled, his eyes glancing towards Jacintha who managed to give Lord Slate an over bright smile as he left the room. She let out a long breath as the door closed behind him, making her father frown.

"Jacintha, you were a little rude there," her father said quietly, gesturing for her to come to sit across from him. "Whatever is the matter?"

"Lord Slate came to see you?"

"Yes, of course he did," her father replied, with a slight frown. "Why would he not? He thought it best to introduce himself, given that he has already called upon you once before when I was not at home."

Jacintha sighed and sat down carefully in the chair, not quite sure how to explain herself. "What did he want?" she asked, worried that Lord Slate had asked her father whether or not he could court her. "Was it merely an introduction?"

"Yes, just that," her father replied, looking more confused than ever.

"He did not ask you anything more than that?" Her heart began to pound, worried that Lord Slate had made more of his introduction than he ought, that he had not listened to her request to become a little better acquainted with him.

"Indeed not, Jacintha, it was merely an introduction," her father reassured her, frowning a little. "I do not understand, however. I thought you liked the man."

Now it came Jacintha's turn to frown. "Where did you hear that?"

"Harmonia has spoken to me of him," he said, with a small shrug. "She is very good at telling me all that is going on."

Jacintha sighed and rolled her eyes, making her father laugh. "I suppose she is very good at keeping you informed, is she not?"

He shook his head, a wide smile on his face. "She has no suitors of her own, Jacintha, although I am sure she would tell me if she did. Harmonia is caught up in her own thoughts about love and matrimony, just as you are."

"I have never wanted a marriage with love and affection, Papa," Jacintha said, slowly, "For I have only ever considered a marriage of convenience."

"And you do not think that Lord Slate is a suitable gentleman?"

The bewilderment on her father's face made Jacintha smile, aware that her own heart was just as conflicted. "I am aware of just how strange this must sound, Papa, but I am not quite sure about Lord Slate. I wish to get to know him better before I consider anything more."

Her father nodded slowly. "That is indeed wise, my dear. Your acquaintance is of short duration, is it not?"

"A sennight, Papa."

"Then I think your plan a wise one, although I would urge you to consider Lord Slate seriously. He is a good man, by all accounts, with wealth and holdings to keep you in

comfort for the rest of your days." Seeing Jacintha's astonished look, the Duke laughed aloud. "My dear Jacintha, did
you not think that I would look into the man the very
moment Harmonia mentioned that he was eager in his
pursuit of you? I may not be able to attend balls and the like
with you, but I have always been determined to do everything I can to aid you in your search for a suitable
husband."

Jacintha felt tears prick at the corner of her eyes,
blinking them away rapidly. Her father, she knew, cared for
them all very deeply and this was his way of showing it.

"You are very dear to me, Jacintha, but I want you to
ensure that this gentleman – or whichever gentleman you
choose – is the right one. Marriage is not something that can
simply be discarded whenever you wish it, so make sure you
choose wisely."

"Thank you, Papa," Jacintha murmured, getting to her
feet and dropping a kiss to his cheek. "You are very good
to me."

He smiled and caught her hand. "You are a wonderful
daughter, Jacintha, never doubt it. Whoever has you for
their wife will be blessed indeed."

As she left the study, Jacintha found herself almost on the
verge of tears. She could not tell whether or not it was
because of her father's kindness or if it was to do with Lord
Slate.

"Jacintha!" Harmonia exclaimed, as she came into the
drawing room. "Did I see Lord Slate coming from father's
study?" Her eyes were wide, an excited smile on her lips but
Jacintha waved her questions away, shaking her head.

"I am not engaged if that is what you are to ask me," she

said, quickly, seeing the smile fall from Harmonia's lips. "And glad not to be, I confess."

Harmonia frowned, sitting back down in her chair. "Oh."

"Lord Slate was just coming to make himself known to Papa."

"Oh," Harmonia said again, still frowning. "And here I thought that...."

Jacintha shook her head, letting out a long breath of relief. "No indeed, and I am glad for it. Only last evening Lord Slate asked if he might court me and I told him no."

"You did?" Harmonia asked, sounding most surprised. "But I thought you liked him."

"I do," Jacintha admitted, sitting down beside her sister. "However, last evening I found him rather forward." Briefly, she described what had occurred, leaving out the part about Henry seeing them. "I told him that I wished to get to know him a little better first, and I am glad to have said such a thing. I think it is best before one commits to courtship."

"Indeed it is," Harmonia breathed, her eyes wide. "I am surprised he took such liberties in the middle of the ballroom."

Jacintha sighed heavily and rested her head on the chair. "As am I," she said, quietly.

There was silence for some moments. Jacintha was caught up in her thoughts, still confused over Henry's anger and Lord Slate's intentions. She had been surprised to see Lord Slate at her father's door, for it felt as though he were staking his claim on her in some way. But, then again, she could not forget that he gave every appearance of a good nature, that he had good conversation and was handsome as well. There was no reason she should not seriously consider him.

But yet, she could not forget the emotions that had risen in her when Henry had taken her in his arms. They had danced the waltz and she had done all she could to try and persuade him that she did not care about him in the least – when the truth was quite the opposite. Her heart had quickened its pace, memories of the times they had spent together pouring into her mind. When he had pulled her a little closer, she had felt herself tremble. There had been no such emotion with Lord Slate.

Giving herself a slight shake, Jacintha gave herself a stern talking to. Lord Slate was quite a charming gentleman and her Papa was quite right to say that she should take his proposal seriously. He had wealth, houses, status and a good family – all in all, everything a Duke's daughter could ask for. And yet, there was still something holding her back.

"By the way, I received a note from Claudia inviting us for tea tomorrow," Harmonia said, breaking into her thoughts. "It arrived earlier this afternoon, and I have not replied yet. I thought to ask you first."

The thought of possibly running into Henry made Jacintha wince inwardly.

"She says that Henry has left home for a time," Harmonia murmured, picking up the note and handing it to Jacintha. "She would like to introduce us to her betrothed, Lord Barker."

"Henry has left home?"

Harmonia looked over at her sharply. "Yes, so she says. I do not know why."

Jacintha frowned and tried to shrug, pretending that it did not matter. "Of course, it does not matter. I was just surprised to hear that he had gone when I only spoke to him last evening."

"Mayhap it was a sudden decision," Harmonia replied.

"Anyway, should you like to go? I think I would like to meet Lord Barker. He has been away on business since we came to London but is back now. I am quite sure Claudia would be more than delighted if we agreed."

Jacintha nodded and tried to smile. "Of course we shall go. I would very much like to meet her betrothed."

"Very good, I shall write back at once," Harmonia declared, with a wide smile. She made her way over to the writing desk by the window and sat to write immediately.

Jacintha let her gaze rove over the room, trying not to think on Henry. She ought not to even be thinking of him when there was so much else going on with Lord Slate, but the fact that he had suddenly left town dogged her mind. Where had he gone? Why had he left so suddenly? She hoped desperately that it was not because of what he had witnessed, although she could not think why that would make him quit London.

Shaking her head to herself, Jacintha sat up a little straighter and resolved to put Henry out of her mind. She would not ask Claudia about him, nor even mention his absence again. She had Lord Slate to think of, for he might very easily become her future, and that was what was most important. She had asked Lord Slate if they might get to know each other a little better and that was what she intended to do. There was no space for any other considera-tion. Her father thought Lord Slate was a good match and his desire was for her to marry and settle. She did not want love - more a marriage of convenience – and Lord Slate offered all of that.

So why was she still thinking about Henry?

CHAPTER EIGHT

*H*enry had not been given any time to settle in. The moment he had arrived at his uncle's home, he had been charged to eat quickly so that they might go out on patrol.

Henry, who was hungry after his long journey, appreciated the plate of good food set in front of him, his stomach growling just a little.

"So, we are to go out on patrol tonight," his uncle said, as Henry began to eat. "I will introduce you to the others."

"What is our aim?" Henry asked, lifting the glass of wine to his lips and taking a long sip. "What if we see a smuggler?"

His uncle chuckled. "They are not so easy to spot as all that! They are aware that we have a patrol and are very careful."

"If they know about it, then why use this spot?"

Uncle Roderick shrugged. "Because it is a good place to smuggle, I suppose. There are a great many caves all along the shoreline, with some you can only reach by boat. We believe that they are putting their goods into one of the larger caves somewhere along the coast and are slowly moving them from place to place until they reach the shore."

Henry frowned. "But then surely you can capture them when they reach the shoreline?"

Roderick shook his head, something like frustration written on his face. "Believe me, we first thought that too. It seemed much too easy – but there has only been the rare occasion when that has happened. Somehow, they are managing to get their goods into the village without us knowing. A patrol is all we can do at the moment, but it is important to be aware of your surroundings at all times. The men will show you what to do and where to go."

Tucking into another forkful of food, Henry felt his spirits lift just a little. He had been rather despondent over Jacintha ever since he had seen Lord Slate kiss her hand in such an intimate manner. That had pained him enough, but then to discover that she thought he would talk about her in order to spread gossip had cut to his very core.

"Something else on your mind?"

Henry looked up to see Roderick looking at him with a slight smile on his face.

"No, not at all," Henry replied, gruffly. "I had a rather unfortunate encounter with a friend before I left London, that is all."

"An unfortunate encounter?" his uncle repeated, frowning. "Whatever does that mean?"

Henry sighed, lifting his shoulders. "It means that I was shown exactly how I appear to someone I once called a friend. It pains me to admit it, but I am not the kind of man I should be."

"But that is exactly why you are here, is it not?" his uncle asked, with a lift of his brows. "You need not concern yourself over that exchange any longer, not when you are going to prove them quite wrong in their estimation of you."

Henry wanted to say that Jacintha had been quite right in her estimation of him, but found that he could not quite say it. Even speaking her name brought him pain.

"Now, the moment you have finished, I must ask you to go upstairs and change," his uncle said, changing the subject entirely. "We must wear dark colors – and be warm as well. It may be the height of summer but the sea air can still be cold, especially at night. I have had my butler lay out some things for you."

"Thank you, uncle," Henry replied, finishing the last of his wine. "I am already looking forward to stepping out on the Dover coast."

His uncle chuckled and rose from the table. "I shall be waiting at the door for you when you are ready, Henry. Do try to hurry, however. The men will be ready soon."

Henry hurried from the table and up to his bedchamber, grateful that there was someone there to assist him. As he drew on the darker clothes, Henry felt something shift inside him. It was as though he was remembering the kind of man he had once been, a man who took his responsibilities seriously. A man who did not shirk from his duties, who did not hide from a challenge. That was the kind of man he wanted to be again.

"And this is the way to do it," he muttered to himself, as he pulled on the long, dark coat over the rest of his clothes.

Clattering down the stairs, Henry reflected on what he might be doing this very moment had he remained in London. Most likely he would be out at some soiree or other, drinking too much brandy and enjoying the flirtations of the less than proper ladies. He would be enjoying every minute of it and not once stopping to think about what impact his behavior was having on others. Much to his shame, he thought of Claudia and her betrothed, hoping that he had not damaged Claudia's chance of happiness.

"You look quite the thing," his uncle declared, as Henry strode towards the door. "Ready?"

"Ready," Henry agreed, a sense of purpose being hoisted onto his shoulders. "Lead on, uncle."

Many hours later, Henry trudged his way back home, feeling tired yet satisfied. He had spent a long time out with the rest of the men and was surprised at how easily they had accepted him. They had welcomed him as though he were an old friend, slapping him on the back and shaking his hand firmly. They were men of all backgrounds, all situations – and yet they worked wonderfully together.

The night had been rather cold, just as his uncle had said, but Henry had managed to keep himself warm by striding along the sands of the long beach that seemed to stretch for miles in one direction before ending at the caves on the other. There had been very little to see, other than the moonlight bouncing off the waves. Henry would have found the whole thing rather boring had it not been for the conversations going on all around him. He had joined in at times, finding that he could make the men laugh simply by regaling them with stories about his time in London. Some questioned why he had left all that to come here, but Henry had merely shrugged and stated he'd wanted to help his uncle.

"So, Henry, how did you find it?"

Henry laughed at his uncle's curious expression. "I

enjoyed it, Uncle Roderick. You need not worry that I shall be so bored that I return to London almost at once."

His uncle grinned, his features lit by the moonlight. "I am glad to hear it."

"But no sign of any smugglers?"

"I wouldn't be too sure about that," his uncle replied, with a chuckle. "There was a boat out on the horizon that we are continuing to watch."

"A boat?" Henry repeated, stopping dead. "I didn't see any boat."

His uncle laughed and slapped Henry hard on his back. "It was your first night, Henry. Don't be so hard on yourself."

Henry paused for another moment before giving a slight shrug and continuing on his way. It was a relief to get inside, the butler ready to take their coats despite the hour.

"I tend to rise rather late," his uncle said, with a small smile. "The staff is aware of this and so they adjust their own working hours. There should be a tray of something in the drawing room for us both, if you would care to join me?"

Henry couldn't help but grin. "So long as there is something like brandy then I shall be more than happy to join you."

"Whisky," his uncle laughed, leading the way. "One of the finest in Scotland, I believe. Will that do?"

"Absolutely," Henry agreed, delighted to find the drawing room already warm with a large fire in the grate and a tray set out on the table just in front of it. Pouring himself and his uncle a dram each, he settled back into the comfortable chair and stretched his legs out in front of him.

"So you think you'll stay for a time, then?"

Henry nodded. "Yes, I think so. You were right about me, Uncle. I don't like to admit it but I feel as though a large number of bricks have fallen on me all at one time, and their weight is enough to make me realize that something is wrong." He let out a sigh, unable to think of anyone but Jacintha. "This friend of mine, from long ago, said a few things that were rather cutting, yet true. That combined with your intervention has brought me to my senses. I need time away from London. Time to find myself again."

"And does this particular friend have a name?" his uncle asked, raising one eyebrow. "I only ask because you have mentioned her on more than one occasion but have not yet told me her name."

Closing his eyes for a moment, Henry shrugged. "Not that it matters, but she is Lady Jacintha, daughter of the Duke of Westbrook. However, it appears that she is much too taken up with Lord Slate to glance at me. She despises me, I think. I am not the man she knew but I will be so again. I just hope Slate does not propose to her in the time I am gone."

His uncle sat up quickly, setting his whisky glass down on the table. "Wait a minute, Henry. Did you say Lord Slate is this lady's intended?"

"Not her intended, no," Henry replied at once, nausea rolling in his stomach as he thought of Jacintha engaged to such a man. "But he is rather attentive."

"Lord Slate – the Earl?"

Wondering why his uncle was so insistent, Henry nodded. "Yes, I believe so. Why?"

His uncle stared at him for a moment before sitting back, a look of astonishment on his face. "Lord Slate, you say? My goodness. The man's estate is by the cliffs, Henry. You would have seen it as you drove in earlier today, although I would not have expected you to notice it."

"I did see what appeared to be a manor house," Henry

said, thinking hard. "I didn't take much notice of it. You mean, Lord Slate's country seat is there?"

"It is," his uncle said, slowly. "At one time, we thought he might have some connection to the smugglers but it appears that we were quite mistaken."

That caught Henry's attention. "You thought he was involved in the smuggling?"

"I did wonder if that was the case, although I am telling you now not to breathe a word of this to anyone," his uncle said, sternly. "It has never been verified, nor has any evidence of the idea come to light. The only reason we thought he might be involved was that his estate is directly above the shoreline. I wondered if there was a way that the smugglers were getting from the shore to his home – for that would be an excellent place to hide the stolen goods, but nothing has ever been seen. And now, since he has gone to London, I cannot believe it is true in the least."

"Mayhap his staff are involved somehow?" Henry suggested, feeling a trifle concerned for Jacintha. "Would he sanction them to work on his behalf?"

His uncle shook his head. "No, it is just more ideas that have come from nothing. We need not worry about him, Henry. It was just interesting to hear you discuss a name I have heard before."

Henry sat back in his chair, mulling over what had been revealed. He knew that he had already taken a dislike to Lord Slate, merely because of his attentions to Jacintha, so it would not be wise to consider suspecting him out of nothing more than antipathy.

"And with that, I think I shall retire," his uncle said, getting to his feet. "Are you going to stay here for a while?"

"I think I shall have another measure of whisky, if I

may," Henry replied, swirling the last few dregs around in the bottom of his glass. "Goodnight, Uncle."

"Goodnight, Henry," Roderick replied. "Thank you for your help this evening. It was good to have your company."

Henry smiled and watched his uncle leave the room before turning back to stare into the flames.

CHAPTER NINE

"Thank you for the carriage ride."

Lord Slate smiled and pressed Jacintha's hand for a moment, his eyes bright. "You are most welcome, Lady Jacintha. I am, of course, always at your service."

She smiled, uncomfortably aware of what he was hoping for. "You are very good, Lord Slate."

"Might I call upon you tomorrow?"

Jacintha paused, aware that he had called upon her almost every day over the course of the last month. He had made it quite clear that he found her more than delightful and was, in fact, deeply committed to her – but still she had not given him the answer he had been waiting for. She could not yet allow him to court her, even though his attentions were fervent. It was as if, the very minute she said yes, she would find herself bound to him forever.

"You hesitate."

She looked up, aware that her focus had been a little distant. "I do apologize, Lord Slate."

He smiled, his expression a little rueful. "You find me too attentive."

"No, it is not that," she exclaimed, the lie rolling quickly from her tongue. "It is just that..."

The words died on her lips. She could not find the words to explain how she felt, despite the conflicting emotions in her heart. What was holding her back? Lord Slate was kind, affectionate and charming. He had good conversation, was quick-witted and often made her laugh. Were she to agree to his court, then she could be assured of a life filled with contentment, for he was not short of coin and had a good title to his name. It would be the marriage of convenience she had been waiting for.

And yet thoughts of Henry held her back.

"My dear Lady Jacintha, you can have no doubt as to the question in my heart," he said, softly. "I long to have you by my side. Will you not allow me to court you? I know your father will give his consent."

"Yes, he would. At once," Jacintha agreed, a little wryly. "You are very good to keep waiting for me to answer you, Lord Slate."

"I hope it shows you the depths of my affection," he replied, pressing her hand to his lips. "I am devoted to you, Lady Jacintha."

She swallowed, her smile a little dry. "Might I give you my answer by the morrow?"

The delight on his face told her that he was truly thrilled at the prospect of finally receiving an answer.

"But of course," he said at once. "I have waited for long enough that one more day will not be too trying."

A flash of guilt raced through her. "Thank you, Lord Slate," she mumbled, her fingers smoothing her skirts in an attempt to calm her nerves. "I am looking forward to it also."

.   .   .

Getting back home was a relief. Lord Slate had been more than attentive of late, showering her with gifts and making his intentions quite clear to every member of the family – and still, she had held herself back. It was foolishness indeed, but her heart would not let go of Henry.

He had been gone a month now and she found herself filled with questions over him. Where had he gone and why? When she had met with Claudia, there had been very little said about him, although Claudia appeared to be rather relieved at his prolonged absence. Jacintha had thought it rude to ask about Henry directly, as well as worrying that she might make herself a little too obvious to speak about him so directly. So, instead, there had been nothing said about him and she had been forced to content herself with that.

"Jacintha? You look rather flustered."

Surprised to find her father in the drawing room instead of his study, Jacintha stopped dead before shrugging and coming to sit near the fire. Her father was evidently feeling the cold today, given the fact that there was a small fire in the grate.

"It is quite warm outside, Papa," she said, quietly, gesturing to the sunlight streaming in through the window. "Don't you wish to go outside?"

"Not today," he said, with a chuckle. "I know you are trying to look after me by suggesting I take the air, but I am growing rather weary with London. Mayhap we shall have to return to the country soon." He tipped his head and studied her. "How would you feel if we were to do so? I know the Season is not anywhere near its end but I am growing quite weary these days."

"You must do as you please, Papa," she said at once,

finding herself almost relieved at the prospect. "You know that Harmonia and I would be happy to go home."

He frowned, his lips twisting just a little "And what about Lord Slate?"

Jacintha cleared her throat, turning her gaze away from her father. "I – I cannot say, Papa."

There was a moment of silence. "He is very attentive towards you, Jacintha. I know he wishes to court you, and you need not fear that I would not give him my consent."

She let out a sigh. "I am more than aware of that, Papa."

"I would see you settled, Jacintha," he said, a little more softly. "If there is something you do not care for when it comes to Lord Slate, you must let me know at once. I will take you home and we can come back to London the following year."

She shook her head, unable to find any excuse for her lack of conviction. "There is nothing wrong with Lord Slate, Papa. I find him quite the match, in almost every way."

"He is a *very* suitable match, Jacintha," her father agreed, studying her carefully. "So what is the matter?"

Jacintha closed her eyes for a moment. It was time to make a decision.

"Nothing is the matter, Papa. He has asked to court me and I shall give him my consent come the morrow."

There was a prolonged pause.

"Very well," her father said, eventually. "I do hope that you are happy and settled with this decision, Jacintha. I do not think that he will wait too long before proposing to you."

Jacintha could not help but agree, the tension she felt slowly draining away as she smiled back at her father. "I agree. He is very ardent and it would not make sense for him to wait with such a proposal."

"And how would you feel about such a thing?" he asked, leaning forward in his seat. "Would you truly be content to be called Lady Slate?"

Henry came into her mind with such force that she caught her breath. Why would he not leave her? Why did he torment her mind, forcing her to consider him when she was making such a big decision?

"I am sure I will be very content, Papa," she replied, pushing the thought of Henry out of her mind completely. "As you said, he is a wonderful match."

The following afternoon found Jacintha and Lord Slate out walking, the brightness of the afternoon bringing a slight smile to Jacintha's face.

"You look very lovely this afternoon, Lady Jacintha," Lord Slate murmured, looking over at her. "In fact, I do not recall you ever appearing so tranquil as you are this moment. Has something occurred? A weight gone from your mind? A decision you have made?"

Jacintha chuckled, trying to glare at him but failing. "You are much too forward, Lord Slate."

"Can you blame a man who has waited for such a long time?" he asked, taking her hand and placing it on his arm. "Come now, Lady Jacintha, do not torment me any longer. Tell me what you have decided."

She paused, waiting until they had passed a few other ladies before looking up at him. "Lord Slate, I do apologize for making you wait for such a prolonged length of time. I will not refuse your request."

He looked at her for a long moment, a slow smile spreading across his face. "Can it be?" he said, softly, his voice so hoarse she could barely hear him. "Can it be that Lady Jacintha has finally accepted my suit?"

"I have," she replied, surprised at how her heart sank at those words. "I do apologize for taking so long to make my decision."

"I would have waited for a lifetime if it were to know that you would accept me in the end," he replied, his gaze so intense that she was forced to look away.

She tried to smile, resuming their slow-paced walk. "I am also troubled to tell you that we may not be long in town," she said, slowly. "My father is not all that well and he has revealed to me of late that he is rather tired. We may have to return to the country estate very soon."

He nodded sagely, his eyes dimming. "I am sorry to hear that."

"It is what is best for my father," she continued, wondering if this sudden change in circumstances would bring about a change in their attachment. "With no mother to speak of, my sister and I can hardly remain in London without a chaperone."

"No, of course not. I quite understand," he replied, with a quick smile. "I am sorry to hear that. There may be something I can do to assist you in that, however."

"Assist me?"

He shrugged and laughed, waving away the concerned look she gave him. "I mean well, I assure you. It is just that I am not particularly inclined to lose your company, not when I have only just been given permission to court you!"

"Oh," Jacintha murmured, still not quite sure what he intended. "I appreciate your desire to help, Lord Slate. Thank you for understanding about my father. As he is the only parent I have left, I am always willing to do exactly what he needs."

"And that is a credit to you," he answered at once, the warmth in his expression never fading. "My dear Jacintha – may I call you Jacintha? – it speaks highly of your character that you show such affection to your father."

Jacintha did not know what to say, finding that his reference to her name without her title to be a little disconcerting. But, then again, they were very close and, given that their courtship would most likely lead to a proposal, a proposal she would have to take seriously, Jacintha could find no harm in it.

"You may call me Jacintha but, of course, only in private company," she said, eventually, when he pressed her hand. "My sister and father will not mind, for example."

"Of course, of course," he replied, looking as though she had granted him some wonderful boon. "And you may call me 'Slate', should you wish to."

It was on the tip of Jacintha's tongue to refuse him, to give him the title he was due, but instead, she simply smiled and nodded, wondering why her heart did not feel as delighted as she had expected.

As they walked, Jacintha only half listened to Lord Slate's conversation, her thoughts entirely on what she had done, what she had committed herself to. She had thought that, in speaking to him and agreeing to his court, she would feel relieved, even happy, but instead found herself despondent. Her heart and her head did not match, fighting one another constantly. How much she despised that!

If only she could forget about Henry entirely! Then things might be so much easier, might be simpler for her. She could choose Lord Slate and be glad about her decision instead of wondering what Henry would say when he found out.

He has probably forgotten all about you, Jacintha, she told herself, as they continued on their way. *Put him out of your mind, just as he has put you out of his.*

CHAPTER TEN

"*C*laudia! How lovely to see you."

Jacintha smiled as her friend rose to greet her, only for the smile to fix on her face as she saw none other than Henry beside Claudia, rising to greet her.

"Henry," she breathed, her gut tightening. "You have returned."

"Good afternoon, Lady Jacintha," he replied, executing a perfect bow. "Indeed, I have returned. I do hope you will not mind me staying here for a brief visit with you?"

"No, not in the least," Jacintha murmured, still rather shocked by his presence. "This is your home after all."

She sat down carefully, relieved that Harmonia was able to continue the conversation without her. There was a lot of discussion about wedding plans and the like but still, Jacintha found she could not quite concentrate on what was being said. The fact that Henry was here had overtaken her completely.

"Are you quite well, Lady Jacintha?"

"Just 'Jacintha,'" she replied, frowning at him. "I thought we did not do titles, Henry."

"I will refer to you in whatever way you wish," he answered, with a lift of his shoulders. "I do not want to displease you."

A little taken aback at his manners, Jacintha blinked once, twice, before shrugging and trying to smile. "When did you return to London?"

"I am only here for a brief visit," he replied, as Harmonia and Claudia continued to converse excitedly about Claudia's wedding plans. "I return to stay with my uncle again in less than a week."

"Your uncle?" Jacintha repeated, wondering who this uncle might be. "I don't think I have ever met him."

"No, you have not," he replied, with a small smile. "My father's brother, the Honorable Roderick Larchmont, lives near the Devon coast. I am assisting him in a small operation there."

For a moment, Jacintha was robbed of speech. This was not the Henry she knew, the Henry she had been so disappointed with. "An operation?"

He smiled, his eyes warm with no trace of the arrogance or anger she had seen there before. "I cannot speak too much about it, but my uncle is involved in attempting to stop a band of smugglers operating near the coast. I thought to help him."

Jacintha was about to speak, when he held up one hand and shook his head. "No, that is not so. The truth is, he told me that I ought to come to stay with him for a time but I did not want to. It was only when I saw myself the way others see me that I decided to change my mind. I have you – amongst others – to thank for that."

Jacintha blinked, hardly able to take in what was being said. Had Henry truly decided to turn his back on his rakish ways? She was not quite sure she believed it.

"I am sure you will be very much looking forward to when your time with your uncle is over," she said, softly, watching him carefully. "The Season will be nearing its conclusion soon and you would not want to miss it."

He shrugged, a quiet laugh escaping from him. "In truth, my dear Jacintha, I find that I could not care less whether or not I miss the end of the Season. Being with my uncle has shown me a great deal about myself and my character and it is something I have determined to change. To take myself away from all that I loved has been something of a challenge, I will admit, but it is not something that I intend to rush back into any time soon. I believe that I need to find the man I was before, back when you knew me. Back when I was sensible and dedicated and focused." He must have seen her frown for he laughed again and shook his head. "I can tell that you are struggling to believe me but I am going to prove it – not only to you but to myself. I suppose I should thank you for your candor and your blunt words to me, for otherwise, I might never have reached this place."

All thoughts of Lord Slate left her mind. Harmonia and Claudia's conversation began to fade, drifting into nothingness. All she saw, all she heard, was Henry.

She could not quite bring herself to believe him, not sure that everything he said was true – yet there was a seriousness in his eyes that had not been there before. It was as though he had begun to change, slowly, into the man she had known all those years ago, the man who had almost kissed her. The man who might kiss her again, would she let him.

She caught her breath at the thought, doing her best to hide her gasp. Heat crept up her neck and into her face, making her blush all the more with embarrassment.

"And can you believe it? Henry has been back in town for three days and, as yet, has not set foot outside of this house," she heard Claudia declare, making Harmonia exclaim in surprise.

Henry chuckled. "You are doing it too brown, sister. I *have* left the house."

"A visit to the tailor and to the bookshop is hardly an outing," Claudia replied, with a small sniff. "What I meant was, you are not going out to all the balls and recitals we have been invited to."

"I mean not to go out to anything during this week," Henry declared, surprising Jacintha even more. "You know that I mean to stick to my word, Claudia."

"Yes, I do, and I am proud of you for it," came the warm reply. "Although I will admit that I did not really believe you at the start of the sennight. It was not like my brother to say such things! I thought he was just being foolish."

"I have had quite enough of being foolish, I assure you," Henry replied, rather firmly. "That part of my life is over."

Jacintha looked over at Claudia to see whether or not her friend was rolling her eyes or the like but found, much to her surprise, that she was looking over at Henry rather affectionately. Evidently, Henry's sister believed him, which meant that Jacintha had very little alternative but to do so herself.

"My goodness, Henry," she murmured, looking over at him. "If I had known my words would have had this great an effect, then I would have said something to you a long time ago!"

He chuckled and shook his head. "I probably would not have listened to you then, Jacintha. It seemed to have all converged at once – you, my sister and my uncle. What must it say about me that it took three people to convince me of my folly!"

Jacintha was surprised to see regret in his expression, watching him as he passed a hand over his eyes, evidently frustrated with himself. Had he truly begun to regret how he had been living? She had heard him speak so proudly of his freedom and now, it appeared, he was realizing that it was no freedom at all. His vices were keeping him prisoner, changing him to their pleasures. This was certainly not the Henry she had first met when she had come to London. When he looked up at her, their eyes meeting yet again, a deep piercing sadness hit Jacintha's soul. She realized just how much she had missed Henry, albeit the Henry she had known all those years ago. To see him now, slowly changing back, brought her a happiness she had not expected.

"You are looking at me rather strangely, Jacintha," he said, quietly, a small smile curving his lips. "Is everything all right?"

Jacintha tried to laugh but it came out as nothing more than a croak. "I am quite well, I assure you. I am just quite taken aback, Henry."

"None as much as I," he replied, with a laugh. "But what of you, Jacintha? What has happened whilst I have been away?"

Jacintha made to shrug off the question, not wishing to talk to him about Lord Slate, when Harmonia piped up, her eyes bright.

"Oh, Lord Slate has been *very* attentive to Jacintha, I must say."

"Lord Slate?" Claudia repeated, leaning forward in excitement. "Goodness, Jacintha! He is a man to be much admired. You should do well if he is inclined towards you."

Jacintha did not know where to look, wishing Harmonia

had not said a thing about him. Seeing Claudia look at her expectantly, she tried to smile and appear as casual as possible, not wishing to draw attention to him.

"He has been very attentive, yes, but we shall see what follows. Papa is not feeling all that well, and so we may soon have to return to the country."

"You need not be so coy, Jacintha, not when we are amongst friends," Harmonia said, looking puzzled. "It is quite all right to state that Papa has given Lord Slate his consent to court you. You appeared quite excited about it only recently!"

Jacintha felt her throat close as she saw the disappointment on Henry's face, which was, after a moment, quickly replaced with a bright smile.

"How wonderful!" Claudia exclaimed, clapping her hands together. "My dear Jacintha, Lord Slate will make a wonderful husband, I am quite sure of it."

Jacintha cleared her throat, holding up one hand. "Do not be too hasty, Claudia. He has not asked for my hand yet."

"But when he does, why would you not say yes?" Claudia asked, sounding slightly confused. "After all, he is courting you now."

Feeling heat rise in her cheeks, Jacintha tried to change the subject. "I take all my decisions with a great deal of seriousness. Now, Claudia, you must tell me all about your own wedding arrangements. They sound quite wonderful, from what I have been hearing."

Thankfully Claudia was more than delighted to talk about her wedding plans and was soon chattering merrily about them. Jacintha was required only to listen, giving her ample time to glance over at Henry who was, much to her dismay, now sitting with a somewhat dejected expression on his face. It cut her to her very heart, wondering if she was the cause of such sadness. Was it because she was now being courted by Lord Slate? Had he hoped that she might turn back to him, to finish what had been started all those years ago? Jacintha closed her eyes and drew in a long breath, before sitting back and trying to listen attentively to all that Claudia was saying. She felt as though she and Henry were engaged in some kind of dance, a dance where they were entirely separate yet longing to draw close to one another. If she spoke to him about how much she had missed him, about how surprised she was at his change in character, would anything come of it?

You have just told Lord Slate that you accept his suit, she told herself, forcing her gaze to remain on Claudia. *Stop thinking about Henry. You have made your decision. Now accept it.*

And yet, no matter how forcefully she spoke to herself, no matter how hard she tried to prevent herself from thinking of him, still her gaze returned to him over and over. Each time, he would look back at her for just a moment before she averted her eyes, telling herself to focus only on Claudia.

Dancing around each other all over again.

CHAPTER ELEVEN

*H*enry could not get Jacintha out of his head. He had traveled back to Ferryway a day earlier than he had intended, simply because it had become almost impossible for him not to appear at her door and demand to speak to her.

He had not known what he would say, of course, even though the scenario had played out in his head a great number of times. He had thought he might ask her to accept *his* suit as well as Lord Slate's, only to realize the foolishness of such an endeavor. He was about to return to the village of Ferryway, she was to go to the country for her father's sake, and he had very little doubt that Lord Slate would follow her there if he could. In fact, he might even propose to Jacintha before she left, such was his apparent ardor! Claudia had waxed on and on about how much of a gentleman Lord Slate was until he could bear it no longer. Of course, he had not told Claudia how much her talk of Lord Slate was affecting him, for he knew she would not understand. In fact, he had spoken to no-one about it, keeping it entirely to himself. After all, who could help him in this matter? He only had himself to blame. Had he been a little more careful about his character and his habits, then he might not now be belatedly attempting to redeem himself in some way.

"You are rather quiet this evening," his uncle commented, as they left the house. "Something on your mind?"

Henry shrugged, wondering if his uncle would understand. "There is something, yes."

"That particular friend of yours?"

Unable to prevent himself from chuckling, Henry grinned in the darkness. "Yes, the very same."

"You saw her?"

"I did."

"And?"

Sighing heavily, Henry looked up to the sky for a moment, taking in the darkness of the clouds. They felt oppressive, as though they were coming to settle all around him.

"She is taken up with Lord Slate," he said, after a long pause. "Lord Slate is apparently the most wonderful gentleman in all of London, according to my sister. She has been rather surprised that Lady Jacintha has taken so long in accepting his court."

His uncle nodded gravely. "I see. And you feel as though you have not the opportunity to prove yourself to this lady."

"We were friends a long time ago," Henry explained, a little exasperated with how foolish he had been. "There was an intimate moment between us, something I have never really forgotten, but we were interrupted before it could come to anything. My father sent me away soon after and we never really saw each other, not until recently."

"And she was surprised at your behavior."

"You know already that it was her words as well as your own that forced me to reconsider my ways," Henry replied. "However it appears as though I will be too late. Lord Slate has intentions for Lady Jacintha and I am sure it will be quite the match."

His uncle was silent for a few minutes, the only sound the crunch of the gravel beneath their feet as they made their way towards the beach. Henry could think only of Jacintha, of how she had looked at him when the revelation about Lord Slate had been made. She had looked almost terrified, as though devastated that he would think ill of her for accepting Lord Slate. It had been a strange look, a strained conversation and yet he could not get it from his mind. She had continued to glance at him as though worried about what he would say and, so, he had chosen to say nothing.

The last thing he had said to her was to bid her good day. It had felt as though he were saying goodbye.

"How very strange that she should be marrying the man whose estate is so close to your own," Henry muttered when his uncle said nothing. "It is as if the universe wants me to see her happy with him, as a punishment for all my foolishness."

His uncle chuckled, breaking Henry's melancholy. "Or maybe it is so that you can ensure she does not do anything foolish," he said, making Henry wonder what he was talking about. "Lord Slate is not a man I have ever been introduced to, but there is something about him that makes people around these parts rather wary of him."

"Wary?"

Roderick nodded. "There is more to tell you about Lord Slate and certainly more to discover. I spoke to some of the men about him, for, as I'm sure I told you, we have some suspicions about him."

A stab of worry kicked Henry in the gut.

"It is nothing serious as yet, but there are some unfortunate instances of the man treating others with sheer disrespect and cruelty." His uncle shook his head, his expression dark. "Not a good man by all accounts."

Henry frowned, thinking hard. This was not the man Claudia had described, surely! His sister was normally a very good judge of character and certainly would not push her friend towards a man who was cruel and unjust! That would certainly not make for a happy marriage.

"That does not corroborate with what Claudia has said about him," he murmured, aware that they were just about to reach the group of men ready to do the patrol. "I am quite surprised to hear you say it, to be honest, uncle."

His uncle smiled, his face lit by the torches the men carried. "I quite understand but not every man is as he seems, is that not so? You have, for example, been playing the fool for a great many months and yet, underneath it all, you are not that kind of man."

Henry flushed, hoping that the darkness hid his change in color. "That is true."

"Then could it not also be suggested that Lord Slate is, in fact, putting on something of a façade whilst he is in London? He needs a wife to produce an heir and so, he is being as charming and as polite as he can in order to secure her." He shrugged, his lips thinning. "After the marriage is over, there will be no need for any more falsehoods."

Something began to crawl through Henry's veins, making him shiver. Was Jacintha truly about to join herself to a man she did not really know? Was he truly this false?

"Here," his uncle said, pointing to one man. "This is Frank. Frank, tell Henry what you know about Lord Slate."

Frank, an older man with a large bushy grey beard, stepped forward, his eyebrows furrowed. "Lord Slate is no gentleman," he growled, his eyes dark with anger. "He tried to have his way with my daughter – by force!" His voice grew loud, his words filled with hate. "Luckily I heard her screaming from the barn and ran to find her. If I hadn't reached there in time, I know he would have forced himself on her."

Henry's heart sank into his boots. Jacintha couldn't know about this side of Lord Slate.

"He warned me not to touch him, else he'd throw me off his land," Frank finished, his hands tightening on the torch he carried. "Lord knows I wanted to do nothing more than finish him off myself, but for the sake of my family, I had to step away. That man's got more power than any one of us, especially over his tenants. What else can we do?"

"And then there's Alfred," Uncle Roderick said, gesturing to another man. "Come on, Alfred. You tell my nephew here what happened to you."

Alfred, a large man, stepped forward, his grim expression matching that of Frank's.

"Lord Slate owed me money," he said, quietly. "I'm the butcher in these parts and don't mind having a tab for the master of the estate. But, after a few months, I expect it to be paid."

"Of course," Henry replied, a little surprised. "Why would you not be paid? It is our duty to ensure that our bills are paid on time, especially to those – "

"Especially to those of a lower class than you," another man interrupted, a knowing look in his eyes. "That's what an honorable gentleman would do. Not Lord Slate."

Henry shook his head, looking back at Alfred. "You mean, he hasn't paid."

Alfred lifted his chin, his gaze steady. "Not only that, but he continues to ask for more meat, still without his previous debt being paid. I don't mind telling you that I've been threatened, more than once, because I've not done what he asked."

"You've held your ground?" Henry asked, his eyes widening. "Goodness, man, that takes some bravery."

"It's not without consequences," Roderick replied, stepping forward. "Alfred here's been beaten black and blue on more than one occasion."

"Knifed me once too," Alfred added, with a small shrug. "Lord Slate's not a good man, Henry."

Henry swallowed and shook his head, his heart filled with concern for Jacintha. "And my friend has caught his eye," he muttered, running one hand through his hair. "I do not believe that anyone in London knows about these things. If there was even a mention of it, I know my sister would not have pushed this particular lady in Lord Slate's direction."

"The man is very good at keeping things hidden," his uncle continued, addressing all of the men by this point. "It is likely, as far as I am concerned, that he may be involved in smuggling. I cannot think of another way for the goods to get from the ships into the village without passing through the estate. We have never seen anything being moved from the shore to the road, nor from the caves to anywhere in the town – and that is even when we have increased our patrols and had some men watching the beach during the day."

"But if Lord Slate is involved, then what is he doing in London?" Henry muttered quietly to his uncle. "And even though his house is right on the clifftop, I cannot see an easy way to get from the sea to his home."

His uncle chuckled, slapping one hand on Henry's shoulder. "And that, my boy, is why we are all here. There is more to discover, more to find. We have to make the connection somehow. There have been smuggled goods found in the village and in the villages beyond – and we need to find out how they got there."

The men chorused their agreement and, with a nod from Roderick, split off into their various groups, ready for the tasks ahead.

"I feel as though I should go back to London, to warn Jacintha about Lord Slate," Henry said, as his uncle fell into step with him. "I cannot allow this to happen."

His uncle shook his head. "I appreciate your fervor, but do you really think Jacintha will believe you without any proof? And what if she were to mention something you said to Lord Slate himself? The game would be up."

Henry's shoulders slumped. His uncle was right. Jacintha would not take his word for it and might easily tell Lord Slate, which would rouse his suspicions and put an end to any investigation.

"Trust me, the best way to help Jacintha to see Lord Slate for who he really is, is to unmask him in whatever way we can. Once we have evidence that he is involved in smuggling – for I truly believe that he is – then we can take the appropriate measures and your lady will be free from his grip. She will see him as he truly is, just as the rest of the world will."

"But what if we do not find any evidence, uncle?" Henry asked, his anxiety only growing instead of dissipating. "What if they are to be wed and nothing is there as proof?"

His uncle chuckled, evidently taking a brighter look than Henry. "Then, Henry, I shall help you object at the wedding itself, where you may scoop up your lady and haul her from the church so that she does not marry Lord Slate. Does that sound quite all right to you?"

"Now you are being ridiculous," Henry muttered, although he could not help but smile. "Very good, uncle, I see your point. Let us hope we find some evidence very soon. I do not know how long I can wait."

CHAPTER TWELVE

"*J*acintha?"

Hearing her sister call her name, Jacintha turned her head as her maid continued to tie back her hair, smiling at Jessica as she came into the bedroom.

"You look very lovely this evening, Jessica."

Her sister grinned, twirling around. "Thank you. One does not need to stop making an effort just because one is married!"

Jacintha frowned, turning back to look at herself in the mirror. "You need not try and give me little hints, Jessica. I am well aware that Lord Slate is dining with us and that we are now courting, but that does not mean that I have decided I will accept his proposal when it comes."

"I see," Jessica murmured, looking rather surprised. "I had thought you had decided on him, Jacintha."

Jacintha shook her head firmly. "No, not in the least. He is pleasant and amiable but I...." She trailed off, heat crawling into her cheeks as she realized what she had been about to say. *I can't stop thinking about Henry.*

There had been such a change in his character the last time they had met that Jacintha had been unable to remove him from her mind. She wondered whether he had truly changed, or whether this was, in fact, some façade of his to try and get under her skin. The fact that he had then disappeared back to his uncle's home without delving back into society when he had been in London had stunned her completely. That was not the Henry she had come to know.

"And you're still quite determined not to marry for love?"

Jessica's question hit Jacintha hard, making her hands clench as they sat in her lap. "I think it is for the best," she managed to say, wondering if she really believed that any more. "There is less difficulty that way."

"I wouldn't agree," Jessica replied, quietly. "There is *more* difficulty, Jacintha. A marriage without love means that you are two strangers, forced to spend some of every day together without the smallest bit of concern or thought for the other. If there is no love then why should you care about what your husband thinks or feels?"

"Because we would be friends!"

Jessica smiled sadly and shook her head. "How long do you think that friendship would last when your husband has to go away on business? When he is so busy with estate matters that he can barely see you?"

Jacintha frowned and glanced over at her sister. "That happens with you and Warwick?"

"Of course it does," Jessica admitted, with a small shrug. "The difference there is that, if he is busy in his study all day, he sends for me so that I might take my reading or sewing into the study with him, simply so we can be in one another's company. If he is gone away on business, I know that I can trust him to return to me with his heart still fully attached to my own."

Jacintha's frown deepened.

"A marriage without love gives no reason for a husband to be attached to his wife," Jessica warned, carefully. "Think hard about what it is you want and why you want it, Jacintha. I can assure you that a marriage without love will present a great many difficulties. That is not to say that if you marry a man who loves you and whom you love in return, that there will not be struggles and times of hardship – but, when those difficulties hit, you will have a reason to fight on together. Do you understand what I am saying?"

"I – I do," Jacintha mumbled, her shoulders slumping. The truth was, she had been questioning all that she had thought already, ever since Henry had made a reappearance in town. She had slowly been pulling away from Lord Slate, even though he had been trying to draw ever closer.

"I hope I did not upset you," Jessica murmured, as the maid stepped away, satisfied with her handiwork. "Come now, we must go. We do not want to keep Lord Slate waiting."

Jacintha followed her sister obediently, her stomach churning just a little. Lord Slate coming for dinner was not something to be worried about, yet she could not help but feel a little anxious. Glad that Jessica and Lord Warwick had agreed to join them, she linked arms with her sister as they descended the stairs, putting all the questions she had over Lord Slate and Henry out of her head for the time being. There would be time later to mull over these things.

"May I say how very beautiful you look this evening, Lady Jacintha?"

Jacintha smiled and nodded, aware that she had not blushed nor felt any kind of heat ripple up her spine. "Thank you, Lord Slate, you are very kind."

He smiled at her again, his brown eyes seeming to warm in the candlelight. Jacintha looked away from him and saw Jessica surreptitiously studying them from across the table - before looking away altogether.

"You have been enjoying the time we have spent together, Lady Jacintha?"

Surprised at his question, Jacintha turned back to face Lord Slate and frowned. "What a strange question, my lord!"

He chuckled, and shrugged, looking a little uncomfortable. "It is, I will admit, but I must know your feelings before I continue with my next question."

Jacintha felt something drop into her stomach, anxiety and nerves filling her. He was not about to propose to her, was he? Not here, not now, surely? Not in front of the rest of her family, not when she would struggle to find a way to tell him that she was not sure. She had swayed in her decision of what she would do should he propose, telling herself that she ought to know her own mind *before* that time came – but now it appeared that she did not yet have a clear answer.

Swallowing, she tried to keep her voice light. "Oh? What question is that, my lord?"

He smiled at her again, a slight gleam in his eye before he cleared his throat and caught the attention of the whole table.

"My Lord Duke, you have been most gracious in allowing me to court your dear daughter, Lady Jacintha. However, I have been dismayed to learn that you are feeling unwell and hope to return to the country soon."

Jacintha's father coughed gruffly. "It cannot be helped, I am afraid, Lord Slate. Although," he continued, his eyes on Jacintha, "if you wished to come and stay for an extended visit, I'm sure that could be arranged."

Her breath caught so quickly in her chest that Jacintha was sure Lord Slate had heard it. She closed her eyes for a moment before lowering her gaze, unable to look anywhere but her hands. The idea of Lord Slate in such close proximity was not one that brought joy to her heart. Why had her father not suggested such a thing to her before now?

"That is very kind of you, Your Grace, and I greatly appreciate such an invitation," she heard Lord Slate say. "But, in fact, I had another suggestion I wanted to put to you."

"Oh"? the Duke replied, lifting a brow. "And what is that?"

Wondering what it was Lord Slate had in mind, Jacintha lifted her gaze to his and saw him smiling broadly at her father.

"Well, Your Grace, I have heard that the sea air is very good for the constitution. In fact, it is highly recommended, I believe."

"So I have heard," the Duke replied, slowly.

"Well, my estate is directly above the sea, on the cliffs of Dover, in fact. I live near the small village of Ferryway and would be truly delighted if you and your daughters would come for a visit."

Jacintha stared at Lord Slate for a moment, her hands tightening as her fingers twined together.

"A visit, you say?" her father boomed, a smile slowly spreading across his face. "Well, that is very generous of you, I must say, Lord Slate."

"Very generous," Jacintha heard herself say, as Lord Slate beamed down at her.

"I was thinking of returning to the country very soon, however," the Duke continued, carefully. "When did you think of returning to your home, Lord Slate?"

"I would be ready to go come the morning, should you ask it of me," Lord Slate replied, carefully. "I am entirely at your disposal, Your Grace, and am truly delighted that you would consider my suggestion."

The Duke chuckled, waving at Jacintha. "I am sure my daughter, in particular, would be delighted to visit with you, Lord Slate. Shall we leave in, say, two days' time?"

Lord Slate beamed. "Capital! I very much look forward to your visit, Your Grace. And to your company, Lady Harmonia and Lady Jacintha."

"I am sure we shall have a wonderful time," Harmonia said, softly, her eyes bright. "Thank you, Lord Slate."

Jacintha felt Jessica's glare from across the table, realizing she had not thanked him for his offer. "Thank you, Lord Slate," she managed to say, putting a smile on her face. "I am already looking forward to seeing your home."

Lord Slate's smile softened as he looked at her. "I am glad to hear it, Lady Jacintha. It is a wild but beautiful place, I confess." He began to wax eloquent on the subject, leaving Jacintha with nothing to do other than to nod and smile, trying to hide the unsettled feeling growing steadily within her heart.

"You do not look altogether pleased with the arrangement, Jacintha," Harmonia said, as they sat to take tea in the drawing room, leaving the men to their port. "Are you still struggling to decide about him?"

Jessica smiled ruefully as she sat down, reaching to pour the tea for the three of them. "I thought he was very kind to offer such a thing to papa, Jacintha, although I can see why it might then be difficult for you."

"It is very kind," Jacintha admitted, slumping in her chair. "I cannot take that from him but I am afraid that he will then propose to me and I still will not know what to say."

Jessica frowned, studying her sister carefully. "I cannot quite understand your confusion, Jacintha. Why not settle on him? What is it about him?"

Knowing she was going to have to be honest, Jacintha sighed and shook her head. "I know Harmonia is aware and I am grateful to you for not saying a word, but I will be truthful with you, Jessica. Lord Musgrove returned to town for a time and I was able to converse with him."

Jessica frowned. "And?"

"And he was like a different creature entirely," Harmonia said, softly. "Very much like the gentleman we once knew."

A look of dawning understanding came over Jessica's face. "I see," she said, quietly. "Then you are caught between affection and suitability."

"Yes," Jacintha admitted, hoping her sister might have some words for her that would bring clarity to her tumbling thoughts. "So what should I do?"

Jessica laughed softly, shaking her head. "My dear sister, it is not for me to tell you what to do or what to say or what to feel – only you can decide these things.

"But whom should I turn to?" Jacintha begged, a feeling of desperation growing within her. "I should not even be considering Henry, for one meeting does not confirm a man's change of character."

"And yet, you cannot stop thinking of him," Harmonia added, with a small smile on her face. "You need not look so surprised, Jacintha. I do live alongside you, after all. It is not as though I cannot see what it is you are struggling with."

Jacintha groaned, putting her head in her hands for a moment. "All I wanted was a simple choice, a convenient marriage. And now I find that I am tossed and pitched in all directions, tormented by my own thoughts. What am I to do?"

Jessica smiled softly, her eyes filled with understanding and compassion. "You are to go to Lord Slate's home, spend time there and decide, once and for all, whether he is the gentleman you want to handfast to for the remainder of your days."

"And what if I decide he is not the man?" Jacintha asked, lifting her gaze.

Jessica's eyes sparkled with good humor. "Then you shall have your answer, my dear sister."

CHAPTER THIRTEEN

"*H*enry? Come quickly!"

Henry sprang to attention, his desire to have a short rest under a rather large oak tree gone in an instant.

"Uncle? What is it?"

"The men have apprehended someone," came the hasty reply. "Hurry now."

Adrenaline shot through Henry's veins as he threw a leg over the horse his uncle had brought him, following his uncle down onto the beach with only the moonlight as their guide. Beyond him, much further along the coast, he could see a few orange lights of the men with torches. There were shouts and cries coming towards him on the wind, making his entire body tighten with anticipation.

"Do we know where he came from?" he shouted, as his uncle rode alongside him. "How did they capture him?"

"Single boat out in the middle of the sea," his uncle replied, his horse trotting along the sand. "They caught him with boxes filled with contraband. I just want to know where he was heading with it all."

Henry frowned, looking over at his uncle. "You mean, he wasn't coming to the shore?"

His uncle shot him a look. "No, of course not. We have patrols here. He was making his way from one of the caves out towards somewhere else, although I don't know where."

His horse tossed his head, clearly feeling the urgency that filled Henry. Some of the caves only filled with water during high tide, which meant that a man with a boat could only get in and out during certain times. But Henry was sure they'd searched as many caves as they could get to, so why hadn't they spotted all this contraband? Where had the man been hiding it?

"I have as many questions as you," his uncle shouted, as they drew nearer the men surrounding the prisoner. "Let's just hope we can get some answers out of him."

Henry threw his reins to another man and jumped down from his horse, striding forward into the crowd to see the smuggler. His heart jumping in his chest, he hurried after his uncle, expecting to see some large, burly man who had been forcibly tied down.

Instead, he saw a small, wiry man with a black eye and a scowl on his face. He had his hands tied behind his back but still remained standing, his short black hair in complete disarray.

"This is the smuggler?" he murmured, as his Uncle Roderick glanced back at him.

"Yes, this is the man," his uncle replied, turning around to dismiss some of the men surrounding them. Waiting until they had gone a short distance away – leaving only himself, the smuggler, Henry and three other men who were guarding the man, he turned back to the smuggler and smiled.

"So, you finally got caught."

The smuggler snorted, his lip curling. "I've got nothing to say to you."

"I think you do," Roderick replied, calmly. "I'm afraid there's a heavy price for smuggling round these parts."

The smuggler did not seem to care, rolling his eyes and sighing heavily. The flames of the torches threw shadows across his face, making him appear almost malevolent. Henry felt himself grow angry at the man's disrespect of his uncle, at his lack of consideration for what he had done in smuggling and stepped forward.

"There isn't going to be an easy way out," he snarled, his hands tightening. "Tell us what we want to know and we might just be able to save you from the gallows."

The man turned his beady eyes on Henry, a mirthful look on his face. "Do you really think the threat of gallows is going to scare me?"

Henry's fists clenched tightly, but his uncle stepped forward, dragging the smuggler's gaze back to him. "I suggest you start talking, my man, otherwise there will be no gallows for you." The sound of a sword being pulled slowly from its scabbard met Henry's ears and the smuggler's smile began to fade.

"I will do what I must to get to the truth from you," Roderick said, slowly, his sword now pointed at the man's throat. "I do not mean to kill you, for that is for the courts, but I will make your life exceedingly painful if you do not talk to me."

Henry watched as the tip of the sword was dragged over the man's throat, leaving a thin line of red. The smuggler's throat worked for a moment, his eyes narrowing as he looked back at Roderick as though wondering whether or not he would truly do as he said.

"I would not question him," Henry said, softly. "He means every word."

The smuggler's eyes lit. "Then, if I talk, you're to save me from the gallows."

Henry snorted. "You're not in a position to – "

"Very well," Roderick interrupted, his eyes fixed on the smuggler. "Tell us what we want to know and I assure you that your life will be spared, although I cannot imagine that prison is a much better prospect."

The smuggler grinned. "At least there's a chance of escaping from that place."

Roderick shrugged, his sword now down by his side. "You have my word as a gentleman. Now, tell me about your contraband. Where were you headed with it?"

The smuggler studied Roderick for a moment, before shrugging. "I'm to take it from one cave to another. I have only done it once before."

"A green boy, then," Roderick muttered, darkly. "Who employs you?"

The smuggler shook his head. "I don't rightly know. We don't use names."

"But there must be a man above you!" Henry exclaimed, wishing he could make the man speak more clearly. "What is his name?"

The man shrugged. "He's just the captain. Like I said, we don't use names."

"Then what's the name of your ship?" Roderick asked, sounding a little frustrated. "Every ship has a name."

The smuggler laughed, shaking his head. "You don't know much, do you? The ship signals us with lights and so on but nothing more than that. It's dark, you see." The mocking tone of the smuggler's voice made Henry want to shake him so hard that his teeth rattled.

"Then where were you meant to be taking the contraband?" Roderick asked, slowly. "Tell me the truth, man, or it will be all the worse for you."

There was a short pause. "I was meant to be taking it to a cave three along from the shore," the smuggler said, quietly. "It has to be high tide so that I can get in with my boat."

"But high tide means the caves will fill with water!" one of the men behind Henry said, sounding astonished. "That's suicide!"

The smuggler snorted with derision. "You don't know much about these caves. Not all of them are as they seem."

"Meaning?" Henry said, surging forward to jab hard at the man's chest.

The man's sharp eyes bored into Henry's. "Meaning that there's more to them than meets the eye."

Henry wanted to ask more, wanted to demand that the man tell him everything, but a sharp look from Roderick stopped him.

"I know that Lord Slate is involved somehow," Roderick said, turning back to the smuggler. "What has he got to do with all this? It cannot be a coincidence that the caves you use are almost directly beneath his estate."

A mulish look came over the smuggler's face, his expression growing resolute. "I can't say I'd know much about that," he replied, firmly. "I do what I am told, and that's all."

"So you're telling us you don't know a thing about Lord Slate's involvement?" Henry repeated, rolling his eyes. "How come I don't believe you?"

Shrugging, the smuggler looked away. "Believe what you want."

"I've heard enough," Roderick declared, firmly. "Take

him away, please. I have a few things to discuss with Henry."

The other men took the smuggler back towards the village, no doubt to hand him over to the authorities, leaving Henry and Roderick standing on the sand.

"There's more that he knows," Henry muttered, thoroughly exasperated. "I know that Lord Slate is involved but the man won't say another word!"

"Unfortunately, that's to be expected," his uncle replied, with a sigh. "Lord Slate is a powerful man and, even though we've promised the smuggler that he won't lose his life, he's probably aware that Lord Slate could arrange for it to happen if he says too much. That's why he's keeping things to himself."

"But you have no doubt that Lord Slate is involved?"

His uncle sighed heavily. "No doubt whatsoever, I'm afraid. The smuggler's reluctance to speak only confirmed it."

Henry ran one hand through his hair, suddenly caught up with thoughts of Jacintha. "I must go back to London and speak to Jacintha at once."

"Are you sure that is wise?" Roderick asked, with a slight frown. "We have nothing concrete."

"But we will," Henry replied at once, a sense of urgency filling him. "And soon, surely?"

Roderick nodded, turning to gaze out across the sparkling waves. "I will have to do another search of those caves, although much more thoroughly. Whatever he meant in saying there was more to them than they appeared means there's something we've missed."

Henry nodded, his stomach churning. "And when can we search?"

"Not until low tide, I'm afraid, and certainly not until

daylight," Roderick answered, rubbing his forehead. "And, on top of which, we must make sure not to alert the rest of the smugglers."

"Won't they know we've caught one of their men?"

"They might," Roderick admitted, "but we have to act with all secrecy regardless. If you are to return to London to speak with Jacintha, then you must do so privately. It would not do for Lord Slate himself to become aware of what we are doing."

"I quite understand," Henry replied, reaching out to shake his uncle's hand. "I shall return to you as soon as I can. It will only be a conversation in London before I come back to you."

"Make sure you rest," his uncle warned, a slight smile playing around his mouth. "I would not have you collapsing on the road!"

Despite himself, Henry chuckled. "No, indeed. Thank you, uncle. I shall see you soon."

Henry chose to take the carriage back to London instead of riding, even though he knew he would be faster on horseback. The truth was, he was so tired that he thought he might fall asleep on horseback so had opted to take the carriage. He had fallen asleep almost at once, despite the worry and anxiety growing within him.

The rumbling of the carriage wheels over the cobbled streets of London woke him at once and, within a few minutes of awakening, the carriage had stopped outside his parents' home. Clambering down quickly, he hurried inside and was greeted by a rather surprised looking butler.

"I appear rather disheveled, I know," he said, grinning at

the butler. "I am not staying, but would appreciate a change of clothes."

"And a bath?" the butler suggested, one eyebrow lifting. "I know journeys can be rather tiring."

Henry paused for a moment, wondering whether he really looked or smelled as bad as the butler was quietly suggesting, before shrugging and agreeing to a bath. After all, he had been out on the beach for most of the night and then had traveled back to London with not a thought for how he looked. He could not appear at Jacintha's door without looking a little more distinguished.

"Thank you," he agreed, making his way up to his room. "That would be wonderful."

A couple of hours later and Henry was washed, dressed and fed and certainly feeling a little more respectable than he had been. The urge to go and speak to Jacintha practically drove him towards the front door – only for the voice of his sister to stop him.

"Henry?"

He turned and smiled, still urgently wanting to excuse himself. "Claudia, good afternoon. Apologies for the short visit but I am only come to speak to Jacintha."

"Jacintha?" she replied, frowning. "Whatever are you talking about, Henry?"

He made to explain, only for her to wave her hand at him and walk towards the drawing room. "Henry, I refuse to have a conversation in the hallway. Do me the dignity of at least coming into the drawing room. I have already asked for a tea tray and do not want my tea to grow cold whilst you give me your strange explanation as to why you have appeared out of the blue."

"Where is mama?" Henry asked, as he reluctantly followed his sister to the drawing room. "Papa is out on business, I presume."

"Mama was out late last evening," Claudia explained, as she sat down. "I do not think she has yet risen, nor do I expect her to either, given that we are to go out again this evening. Papa has gone to meet with his solicitor."

"Nothing too important, I hope?"

She smiled, her eyes twinkling. "Just the matter of my dowry, I believe," she replied. "You are going to come to my wedding, aren't you?"

"Of course I am," Henry replied, a trifle impatiently. "Now, Claudia, I meant what I said when I told you I was here to speak to Jacintha. It is a trifle urgent."

"Well, you will not find her here," Claudia replied, making his heart sink. "She is gone."

He swallowed the lump of disappointment. "Gone where?"

"To the country," Claudia replied, airily. "I mean, I think she will be gone by now. They were due to leave this morning and I do not think anything will have held them up."

Groaning, Henry put his head in his hands. "Gone?" he muttered, his frustration mounting. "And the Duke's estate is a few days travel from here!"

Claudia laughed, making him lift his head. "No, she has not gone home, although I believe that was the plan. I received a note from Harmonia yesterday informing me that Lord Slate had invited them all for an extended visit to his home – although I am sure you can imagine why he might do such a thing!"

A wave of nausea rolled in his stomach.

"They have gone to Dover?"

"To the Slate estate in Ferryway, yes," Claudia replied, the smile slowly fading from her features. "Only this morning, of course."

"They *all* went?"

Her sister stared at him as though he had gone mad. "Of course all of them! The Duke would hardly allow his daughter to attend the Slate estate on her own now, would he? Goodness, Henry, what has come over you?"

Henry closed his eyes, not quite sure what to say. He cared for Jacintha more than he wanted Claudia to know and now to hear that she had gone to Lord Slate's home had been like a kick to his gut. "At least she will be nearby," he muttered to himself, looking up at his sister. "Claudia, I must return to our uncle's home."

"Back to Dover?" she replied, suspiciously. "Henry, whatever is the matter? Why are you chasing Jacintha from here to there and back again?"

"I cannot say," he replied, haltingly. "Only know that Lord Slate is not the man he appears to be."

Claudia frowned, her eyes fixed on him. "Henry, you are not quite making sense. I will admit that your change in character has been a welcome one but you are now appearing to be a little obsessed!"

"I care for Jacintha," he said, bluntly. "She does not know Lord Slate's true nature and I must inform her of it."

Claudia's mouth fell open. "What are you talking about? You have not cared tuppence about Lady Jacintha in as many years and now, since she returned to town, you are telling me you cannot get her from your mind? That makes very little sense, Henry. In addition, I thought Lady Hereford might be the one to – "

"I do not care for Lady Hereford," Henry interrupted, slicing the air with his hand, frustration evident in his expression. "She is not the kind of woman for me, even if she is rather keen to deepen our acquaintance. Do not encourage her, I beg of you. You must leave that alone, Claudia, please." He got to his feet, came over to her and dropped a kiss on her cheek. "I know you are only wanting the best for me, but I promise you now that I will never care for Lady Hereford. Do excuse me. It seems I must now return to Dover."

He did not wait but left the room at once, his concern for Lady Jacintha growing steadily. He was not quite sure what would happen once he returned to Ferryway but surely there would be a way for him to speak to Lady Jacintha, even if it meant calling on Lord Slate! She had to know the truth about him. She had to know that he was not who he appeared to be. He had to save her from Lord Slate.

CHAPTER FOURTEEN

"*I*ndeed, I am delighted to have you all here!"

Jacintha tried to smile as Lord Slate lifted his glass in a toast, far too aware of just how much the man had drunk. They had only arrived that very afternoon and, instead of excusing themselves to take tea in the drawing room in order to leave Lord Slate and their father to their port, Lord Slate had insisted that they remain. The tea had been drunk and, much to Jacintha's displeasure, the conversation was becoming a little more ribald. In fact, she was quite astonished at just how different Lord Slate appeared to be. Gone were the gentlemanly manners and careful speech. Instead, there appeared to be a rather easy manner – a little too easy, perhaps – and a slightly drunken slur to his words. This was not the best impression he could have made.

Not that it appeared to matter to her father who was, at this point, enjoying just as much port as Lord Slate. He lifted his glass in return and chuckled, leaning heavily back in his chair. "Thank you for your invitation, Lord Slate. I am sure I speak for both my daughters when I thank you for your generosity."

"Indeed," Jacintha murmured, throwing a glance towards Harmonia who, much to her relief, seemed as perturbed as she. "Papa, don't you think it's time you retired? You have been very tired of late."

The truth was, whilst she was indeed concerned for her father, Jacintha did not particularly want to be in Lord Slate's company at this point. He appeared much too brash for her liking, which rather unsettled her.

"Yes, I agree, Papa," Harmonia added, getting up from her chair. "Do excuse us, Lord Slate, but we are all quite tired from the journey. I hope you do not mind if we retire early."

"Not in the least," he said, getting up from his chair and giving her a slight bow. "I look forward to your company again tomorrow."

Jacintha caught her breath as Lord Slate trained his gaze on her, feeling as though she were being caught in a trap she had not been aware of.

"I shall retire also," she murmured, coming around to help her father from his chair. "Good evening, Lord Slate. Thank you for a wonderful time thus far."

The lie fell from her tongue easily as she took her father's arm and, managing to avoid Lord Slate's gaze entirely, both she and Harmonia helped their father from the room. He was not particularly drunk, however, but rather appeared to be very tired from the trip. The liquor did not help his exhaustion, of course, and Jacintha was relieved when they made it to his bedchamber.

"He has his manservant waiting for him," Harmonia murmured, ensuring that he sat down by the fire in his room before hurrying back towards Jacintha. "We need not worry about him until morning."

"I do hope the journey was not too trying," Jacintha replied, quite concerned for her father's health. "Do you think he will be all right?"

"I am quite sure he will," Harmonia replied, firmly, patting Jacintha's arm. "You need not worry. After all, this trip is mostly about you and your future, is it not?"

Jacintha sighed, chewing on her bottom lip for a moment. "Yes, I suppose it is."

"You were not pleased with Lord Slate's behavior this evening?"

"I was surprised," Jacintha admitted, quietly. "Mayhap he is just glad to be home again and has allowed himself a trifle more freedom. You know how it feels to return to where you belong."

Harmonia nodded, her eyes searching Jacintha's for a moment. "The future is not decided, Jacintha," she said, softly, with one hand on the door handle to her bedchamber. "Remember that."

Jacintha smiled and pressed a quick kiss to her sister's cheek before bidding her goodnight. Walking quickly along the corridor towards her own bedchamber – which, much to her confusion, was quite a distance away from her sister and her father's rooms – she tried not to worry about Lord Slate's strange behavior this evening, putting it down to good spirits and nothing more.

"Ah, Jacintha."

She shrieked, jumping back in fright as Lord Slate himself appeared at the top of the staircase to her right, holding onto the rail with one hand and with a glass of port in the other.

"Lord Slate," she gasped, putting one hand on her frantically beating heart. "Whatever is the matter?"

"Nothing is the matter," he replied, with a wide grin. "I just wanted to ensure that you were quite well before you retired to bed." He climbed the remaining two stairs and came towards her, staggering just a little. "Are you quite well, Jacintha?"

"I am," she replied, glancing along the hallway and wondering how she was to get around him in order to reach her bedchamber. "You need not worry yourself, Lord Slate."

His smile was slow, turning into a leer as he moved infinitesimally closer. Warnings began to sound in Jacintha's mind, making her lurch away from him, only for him to grasp at her arm.

"You need not run from me, Jacintha," he murmured, his eyes growing dark as he pressed her back against the wall. "This will be your home one day soon. You have nothing to fear from me."

"I do not fear you," she replied, firmly, despite the fact that she did not feel as assured as she sounded. "But I would ask you to release me, Lord Slate. I am tired and wish to go to bed."

"Would you like me to accompany you?"

She gasped, her eyes widening as he grinned, his eyes fixed on her lips. The question was so rude, so uncouth, that she did not know what to say.

"I assure you that there is nothing wrong in partaking in such things before we are wed," he whispered, as though to encourage her to do exactly what she knew she should not. "A few months in advance will be of very little consequence."

"No, my lord," Jacintha said, as strongly as she could. "I do *not* wish for such a thing."

This is not Lord Slate, her mind screamed, as she tried to move away from him towards her bedchamber. *This cannot be the man who courted me so patiently in London.*

Lord Slate sniffed, the smile slowly fading from his face. "That is rather disappointing, Jacintha. After all, I have been very patient with you thus far. Is it any wonder that I am growing impatient now?"

She swallowed, a curl of fear growing within her. "You forget, Lord Slate, that you have not proposed, nor have I accepted."

He snorted. "What does that have to do with it? You are well aware of my intentions, and I hope you would not have granted my court without being aware of what I wanted from you."

Jacintha winced as he grasped her arm a little more tightly, pain shooting through her. "Lord Slate," she said, still trying to remove herself from him. "You are hurting me."

He did not appear to hear her. "Perhaps just a taste of what you can expect will help," he mumbled, stepping so close to her that his body was pressed against hers. "After all, you have never so much as kissed me."

Everything in her rebelled at the idea. She did not want to kiss him, did not want to press her lips to his. She felt nothing but fear, wanting to escape from him, to run from him. His hands tightened on her arms, forcing her to stay in place.

His lips were wet, trailing down from her cheek to her mouth. Shuddering, Jacintha turned her face away – and he paused.

"What is the matter?" he asked, sounding rather angry. "We are to be husband and wife, this is what you should expect."

"I will never expect to be treated in such a way," she whispered, pressing the side of her face against the wall in an attempt to keep even her gaze from his. "Let me go, Lord Slate."

There was a long silence. His grip did not lessen nor did he move away. Jacintha remained exactly as she was, ready to twist away from him the moment he let her go.

"You will do everything I ask of you, and more," Lord Slate hissed, eventually, pressing the length of his body against hers. "You had better learn to obey, Jacintha, for I am warning you now that I do not take kindly to disobedience."

She turned back to him then, something like anger growing within her despite the cloying fear. "I do not expect to marry a man who will treat me like one of his servants."

He caught her chin with his hand, squeezing her cheeks painfully. "You will do as you are *told!*"

With such a declaration, he pressed his lips to her again, his hands leaving her arms and making their way down her body – and Jacintha seized her opportunity.

Pushing him, hard, she made to slip past him, only for him to catch her hand. Without thinking, she struck out at once, her hand slapping him firmly across the face. He staggered back and she bolted at once, her soft slippers sliding across the polished floor.

By the time she reached her bedchamber, he had recovered himself and was coming striding towards her. She did not hesitate but opened the door and slammed it, hard, her fingers trembling as she turned the key in the lock. His fists battered on it for a moment, vile curses springing from his throat – and Jacintha trembled with every word spoken.

"You will *not* refuse me," he shouted, his words ringing all through the hallway. "I will have my bride. You are the one I have chosen, Jacintha. You will not turn away from me now."

"There is nothing between us any more, Lord Slate," Jacintha replied at once, trying to inject some confidence into her voice. "What was between us is now dead and gone. I fully intend to leave your house as soon as I can."

He chuckled darkly, making shivers run down her spine. "You may well wish to do so, my dear Jacintha," he said, still speaking to her through the door. "But mayhap your father can be easily convinced to think otherwise."

Jacintha did not say another word, clamping her mouth shut as he left her. Sliding down to the floor, she buried her head in her arms, leaning heavily on her knees. She had not expected this. She had never once thought that Lord Slate would turn into such a terrifying ogre of a man once they stepped into his home. Was it the liquor that had done so? As much as she hated what had happened, Jacintha felt awash with relief that she had seen Lord Slate's true self – liquor or no liquor. She had meant what she said – she would not stay here, not when there was no chance of a future for them both. Lord Slate would not have her hand in marriage and certainly would never have her heart.

Now it became clear why her bedchamber had been so far from her sister's. Lord Slate had planned to take her here, to make her his own before he had even proposed – possibly even by force. He was a man used to getting what he wanted, it appeared, and that meant that her refusal was more than he could bear.

"I will not be yours, Lord Slate," Jacintha whispered to herself, slowly getting to her feet and making her way towards the bed. "Never, I swear to you."

As she lay down, still fully clothed, her thoughts returned to the one man who had dogged her mind ever since she had last seen him in London – Henry. She knew he would never treat her in such a way, not even when he had been at his worst. For a moment, she found herself wishing he was here with her, keeping her safe from the monster she had not expected to meet. Closing her eyes, she fought tears, wishing desperately that she had never consented to come, that she had listened to her heart and chosen to follow it. If she had, then she might not be stuck in such a difficult situation, she might be back in London hoping that Henry's change in character had been a permanent one.

Jacintha struggled to catch her breath, realizing just how foolish she had been. In her determination not to complicate her life with such things as love and affection, she had pushed away the one gentleman she had never been able to forget and had followed the footsteps of a gentleman she had deemed suitable, only for him to turn out to be anything but that.

How had she managed to make all the wrong decisions? And why had she not seen it before?

Her heart aching, Jacintha gave in to her tears and allowed herself to weep, her world coming crashing around her shoulders. She felt more alone than she had in a long time, her misery wrapping around her like a shroud. She could only hope that her father would be as horrified as she and that, come the morrow, they would be on their way back to London.

CHAPTER FIFTEEN

*D*espite the fact that she had locked her door and shoved a few solid looking chairs against it, Jacintha did not sleep well. She tossed and turned for most of the night, caught by the pain of what she had done, confused over Henry and horrified by Lord Slate. By the time morning came, she was already thinking about packing her things.

Unfortunately, the maid arrived with her breakfast tray as well as a note from Harmonia, which Jacintha read at once. It was brief, asking her to come to Harmonia's chamber as soon as she was ready – although it did not say why.

Instructing the maid to take her breakfast tray to Harmonia's room, Jacintha dressed hurriedly with the help of her maid and quickly made her way along the corridor, trying her best not to feel the swirl of panic in her chest as she passed the staircase where Lord Slate had been only the day before.

"Harmonia?"

Her sister looked up at once from where she sat, her breakfast tray in front of her.

"Sit, please," she said at once, gesturing for the maids to go. "I am glad you are here, Jacintha. Father has taken ill."

Jacintha stared at her sister as the maids closed the door, before coming to sit down opposite her.

"It is nothing too serious, I assure you," Harmonia continued, quickly. "You need not look so concerned. I think that it is nothing more than being overtired as well as partaking in too much liquor. You know how that makes his gout flare up."

Letting out a long breath, Jacintha closed her eyes and leaned back in her seat. The dawning realization that they would not be able to leave Lord Slate's home any time soon crept over her, making her stomach tighten with anxiety.

"I know this is rather trying, but he will be better in a few days," Harmonia continued, when Jacintha did not reply. "Besides, I am sure that you and Lord Slate will be able to get to know one another better."

"Lord Slate and I have no longer any association," Jacintha replied, hoarsely, opening her eyes to see Harmonia's astonished face. "He was most uncouth last evening, Harmonia."

Her sister blinked, shaking her head. "I am aware that he was a little coarse last evening, Jacintha, but I do not think that there is any reason to – "

"Lord Slate followed me to my room last night," Jacintha interrupted, leaning forward to capture her sister's gaze. "He – he tried to...." She trailed off, rather ashamed to admit what had occurred. "I do not understand it," she finished, her voice nothing more than a breathy whisper. "I thought I knew him, but he clearly is a different person than anyone thought."

There was a brief silence, where Harmonia sat forward in her chair and reached for Jacintha's hands. It was only then that Jacintha realized she was shaking, the concern in her sister's eyes making her realize just how truly awful Lord Slate's behavior had been.

"We must leave at once," Harmonia whispered, her cheeks paling. "He cannot be allowed to treat you in such a way!"

"I had hoped to convince father to leave at once, but now he is ill, we cannot risk it," Jacintha replied, shivering just a little as she realized that she was now fully without any kind of protection. "Oh, Harmonia, what have I done? I thought I knew him so well."

Harmonia shook her head, her hand tightening on Jacintha's. "This is not your fault, Jacintha. Lord Slate hid his true nature behind a façade in London and given that he clearly believes he has captured your affections – or at least, our father's consent, he need not pretend any longer."

"Or maybe it was the liquor that forced him to come out from underneath his layered mask," Jacintha muttered, passing one hand over her eyes in an attempt to control her tears. "I want to leave this place, Harmonia, but I feel as though we are trapped here for the time being."

Her sister sat back in her chair, frowning as she thought hard. "Then we shall both simply tend Papa."

"I do not believe he will accept that," Jacintha replied, shaking her head. "Not when he believes that we are all but betrothed."

"It does not matter what he believes," Harmonia said, firmly. "We can simply state that Papa requires us and that will be that. When it comes time to dine with him, we shall do so together and I shall accompany you back to your room. You will not need to be alone unless he has gone from the house for whatever reason."

A slow sense of relief began to fill Jacintha, appreciating Harmonia's sensible and calm decisions.

"I believe he has already gone out this morning," Harmonia finished, sitting back. "Papa is resting also. If you wished to rest a little more, then I will send the maid to fetch you when Papa awakens – or if Lord Slate returns."

Glad that they had brought their own maids with them, Jacintha let out a long, slow breath, already feeling more settled. "That is a good idea, Harmonia – I confess that I did not sleep well last evening."

"Then go and rest," Harmonia replied, "And ensure your maid knows to wake you should Lord Slate return."

Jacintha had enjoyed the rest of her breakfast with her sister and had benefitted greatly from returning to her bed for an hour or so. However, now that she had risen for the second time – and on being assured that Lord Slate was still gone from the house, Jacintha thought she might go in search of the library, thinking to find a good book for both herself and her sister to read whilst they waited for their father to recover. Giving her maid strict instructions to find her should Lord Slate's horse be seen returning to the estate, and telling her that she intended to find the library – which, unfortunately, the maid could not assist her with, Jacintha set off on her exploration. The worry and anxiety she had felt only earlier this morning was already beginning to lessen.

There were a great many rooms in Lord Slate's home, although there were dust covers on quite a few of his belongings. Evidently, the house was not always in use, as though he did not often have guests or the like visiting him. She did not find any staff about, which in itself was rather surprising, forcing her to open the door of each room in order to find the library

Having made her way to the first floor, she quietly made her way from room to room, wondering if she might find out more about Lord Slate. He was not the man she had thought, which meant she knew very little about him. She did question how he had managed to hide his fierce anger and his determination to get what he wanted so well, shaking her head that she had been so easily duped.

Turning the handle of yet another door, she looked inside, only to see shelves of books lining the walls, making her sigh with relief. Stepping inside, she closed the door firmly behind her, relieved to see that the windows over-looked the front of the estate. She should be able to see Lord Slate's return and hide herself from him before he came back into the house.

Brushing her fingertips lightly along the row of books, Jacintha stopped at one particular row, reading the titles quickly but finding nothing to interest her. Continuing to wander along the length of the room, she paused to pick up a novel of some kind, thinking that Harmonia might like to read it. There was another novel underneath, which, at first glance, appeared to be some kind of grisly murder. With a slight shudder, Jacintha replaced it hurriedly, banging her elbow into a small portrait on the wall by the bookshelf in her haste.

Something creaked behind her.

A jolt of fear had her clinging to the shelf for a moment, terrified that Lord Slate had somehow returned and was coming towards her but, without the sound of footsteps, that worry quickly died away. Turning around, she saw that, much to her astonishment, that part of the wall on the opposite side appeared to have come away.

Slowly moving towards it, Jacintha placed the book in her hands down on the table, her heart beginning to pick up its pace as she drew near. Her fingertips ran down the length of the wall, realizing that it was a door.

It was not particularly unusual for manor houses to have secret passages or priest holes within them, so it did not surprise Jacintha all that much – although she could not help but acknowledge the spark of curiosity. Finding a candle on the mantlepiece, she lit it quickly and, without hesitating, opened the door and stepped inside.

Much to her disappointment, the passage did not seem to go anywhere. She took a few short steps inside, only to come face to face with a blank wall. There was no other door as far as she could see, and the only thing she could discover was a trapdoor that was locked with a key.

The key was still in the lock, however, and Jacintha hesitated, wrestling with the desire to unlock it and see what lay beneath. Bending down, she studied the lock and key for a moment, realizing that they were neither rusty nor fragile. This place had been used recently. Looking around the trapdoor a bit more, she saw one wooden box in the corner of the tunnel, hidden by the darkness. It was covered with a cloth and, making to lift it, Jacintha felt a rush of anticipation.

When a sudden whisper met her ears, she dropped the cloth. Hurrying towards the door she looked carefully back into the library, seeing her maid searching for her.

"Has he returned?" Jacintha asked, hurriedly putting the candle back on the mantlepiece and blowing it out before ensuring the secret door was closed tightly.

"Yes, my lady," the maid replied, who still appeared a

little confused as to why her mistress was avoiding the gentleman who had been courting her for so long.

"Thank you," Jacintha said, quickly making her way back towards the door. "If anyone asks where I am, tell them that Harmonia and I are tending to our father, although we intend to dine with Lord Slate for dinner."

"Of course," the maid replied, coming behind her. "I quite understand, my lady."

CHAPTER SIXTEEN

"*U*ncle Roderick!"

Roderick looked up the moment Henry walked into the drawing room, a bright smile immediately jumping onto his face.

"My goodness, that was a rather brief visit to London, was it not? Whatever are you doing back?"

"I have to see her."

His uncle frowned, his expression a little more grave. "See who?"

"Jacintha."

"I thought that was who you went to London to see," his uncle replied, slowly, rather confused. "What are you talking about, Henry?"

The words came out in a rush, betraying the anxiety that had been dogging him ever since he left London. "My sister informed me that Lady Jacintha, her sister and her father have all been invited to Lord Slate's estate here in Ferryway."

His uncle's expression grew astonished. "Lord Slate has returned, then?"

"He must have done so," Henry answered, beginning to pace up and down the room. "Have any of your men seen him?"

"Not that I am aware of," Roderick replied, "But, then again, they have been caught up with this smuggler and searching the caves."

Henry stopped his pacing for a moment, recalling that they had been waiting for low tide. "And?"

"And they found quite a few things," his uncle replied, solemnly. "Sit down, Henry, and I will explain everything to you. You are making me tired simply watching you pace up and down!"

Feeling even more anxious than before, Henry did as he was asked and sat down, leaning forward and clasping his hands together. His uncle got up and poured them both a snifter of brandy, handing him one before resuming his seat.

"My men were only able to search the caves a few hours ago," he began, quietly. "They did not find anything in particular – no contraband, I mean, but there was something of particular interest."

"What?" Henry asked, taking a sip of his brandy and enjoying the way the warmth spread all through him. "Something linking it all to Lord Slate?"

Roderick nodded slowly. "We think so. There is a passageway cut high into the rock."

Henry blinked, quite confused about what his uncle had said. "A passageway? How can that be?"

"Believe me, I was as confused as you until I saw it for myself," his uncle chuckled, shaking his head. "Little wonder we didn't discover it until now. It can only be accessed at high tide, although obviously before the sea reaches its turning point. There is a short window of time when a boat can be sailed into the cave, with supplies then taken into the passageway."

"But what should happen if the tide were to become any higher when the operation was underway?" Henry asked, frowning hard as he tried to make sense of what his uncle said. "Surely the men would be trapped?"

His uncle shook his head. "They could easily climb further into the passageway, and I suspect that that is actually what occurs. One man steers the boat, whilst the other puts the contraband into the passageway. When the boat leaves, the man in the tunnel remains and carries the contraband further into the tunnel."

Nodding slowly, Henry tried to make sense of what he had heard. "So then where does the tunnel lead?"

"That is the most frustrating part," his uncle replied, with a shake of his head. "There is a trapdoor much further along – for the tunnel leads quite far up and along within the cliff walls themselves, but then we cannot go any further. It is locked and bolted from the other side."

"And you think it goes to Slate's manor house."

"I don't think, I know," Roderick replied, gravely. "There's nowhere else it could lead."

Henry blew out a long breath, his anxiety rising. "And now Jacintha is in there, as is her sister and the Duke."

"I do not think she is in any kind of danger if that is what concerns you," Roderick said quickly, wanting to reassure Henry. "Why not go up and ask if you can call on them? I am quite sure that Lord Slate would welcome you, given that you are a friend of the family."

"Do you think so?"

"It would be quite rude of him if he did not," Roderick said, with a half-smile. "I'll come with you if you like."

"Can we go now?"

His uncle chuckled. "I think we must, or it will be too late for calling on anyone."

Awash with relief and hope, Henry hurried from the house, glad that his uncle had suggested such a thing. If he could only speak to Jacintha, then he would be able to inform her of what he and his uncle had uncovered about Lord Slate. It might be difficult to talk to her alone, but he would try and manage it somehow. Waiting impatiently for his horse to be saddled, Henry looked along the hillside to where the Slate estate sat, determination growing in his heart. He would reach Jacintha and tell her the truth about Lord Slate. Even if she did not turn to him, even if she did not want to hear of the affection he had for her, then he would be glad that her association with Lord Slate would be at an end. All he wanted was her best.

Rapping sharply on the front door, Henry lifted his shoulders and stood tall, clearing his throat gruffly as the butler answered it at once.

"Viscount Henry Musgrove," he said smartly, handing the butler his card. "And the Honorable Roderick Larchmont. We hear that Lady Jacintha, Lady Harmonia and the Duke of Westbrook have come for a short visit and would very much like to greet them."

The butler held the door open and Henry and Roderick stepped inside.

"Please do wait here for a moment," the butler intoned, giving them a slight bow. "I shall return in a moment."

Henry let out a long breath, his eyes roaming around the ornate hallway and marble staircase. Lord Slate clearly had a beautiful home, with plenty of space to store contraband, if he was actually using it for smuggling.

"You see?" Roderick murmured, as the butler came back towards them. "His swift return means that they will be vastly glad to see you, I am quite sure."

Hope zoomed into Henry's chest, making him smile broadly as the butler drew near.

"I am very sorry, my lords, but the master and his guests are currently unavailable."

The smile died on Henry's face at once. "Unavailable?" he repeated, looking at the butler in astonishment. "Whatever do you mean?"

"I mean, they are indisposed," the butler replied, with a small incline of his head. "I am very sorry, my lord. Perhaps tomorrow."

"Perhaps tomorrow?" Henry spluttered, about to shove past the butler and hurry into the house in order to find Jacintha. "What are you talking about, man?"

"Henry," Roderick murmured, putting one hand on Henry's shoulder. "Come now. We must go. It would be rude to remain when we have not been invited in."

Henry shook off his uncle's hand, his anger rising steadily. "What on earth can have indisposed them so much that I am unable to see them?"

The butler lifted his chin, a taut line around his mouth. "My lord, the Duke of Westbrook is unwell and both his daughters are attending him. Lord Slate is, of course, caught up with business given that he only returned to Ferryway yesterday." His jaw set, his eyes flashing just a little as he inclined his head yet again. "I *do* hope you understand, my lord."

Henry was forced to step back, his anger spiraling away.

"Come on, Henry," Roderick said again, grasping his arm. "Do give our regards to the Duke and his daughters, as well as Lord Slate," he continued, addressing the butler as

Henry turned away from the house. "And tell them that we will call again in a few days once the Duke recovers."

"Of course," the butler replied, as calmly as ever. "Thank you, my lord."

Henry did not know what to think as he left the house, torn between believing that the Duke was, in fact, ill and unable to see them or thinking that Lord Slate was deliberately keeping them away from Henry.

"Walk slowly," Roderick murmured, as they stepped out of the house. "Give no appearance of anger or frustration."

He laughed aloud, slapping Henry on the back who looked at him askance.

"We must appear to be quite at our leisure," Roderick murmured, as Henry continued to glower. "Give the man no indication that we are in the least bit troubled by these turn of events."

With an effort, Henry shook the tension from him and tried to smile, recalling that they were doing their best to keep Lord Slate completely unaware of their investigation into him. He allowed Roderick to speak rather loudly, his jovial tone still grating on Henry's nerves as they approached their waiting horses.

"Mount and turn the horse in a circle, so that you face the house for a moment," Roderick said, as he pulled himself into the saddle. "And for goodness sake, smile."

Hating that he had to put on such a façade, Henry did as his uncle asked – only to freeze in his seat as he saw none other than Lady Jacintha looking out at him from one of the windows.

The urge to race towards her was stronger than ever before.

"Don't."

His uncle's fierce whisper met his ears, forcing Henry to look away.

"I can see her too but you *must* ride away. Lord Slate cannot know that we are worried about their presence in his home. You have come to call on them and that is all. Please, Henry, do as I ask."

With an effort, Henry turned his horse and began to follow Roderick down the estate path, devastated that he had to leave Jacintha behind. She had not been smiling when he had caught her gaze, nor had there been any happiness in her expression. Was that because she was glad to see him leave? Mayhap she did not wish to see him, mayhap it had been her own wish to send him away.

A heavy weight settled in his stomach, bringing him nothing more than torment and pain. Spurring his horse to a gallop, he rode out past the gates that led to the estate and then down towards the beach, the horse's hooves kicking up sand as he went. Roderick was right behind him, clearly aware of his frustration.

"You ought not to have shouted at the butler," Roderick said, as Henry pulled his mount into a trot. "I know you are desperate to see her but such a reaction will only arouse suspicion."

"I need to see her," Henry replied, looking out at the sea and trying to calm himself down. "What am I to do if he will not allow me into his home?"

"Then you simply try again," Roderick replied, simply. "Give it a couple of days and, in the meantime, remember that we are doing all we can to try and apprehend the smugglers. It may be that, in doing so, we find a way to reveal Lord Slate's true nature to her regardless of your intervention."

Whilst that was true, it did not bring Henry a great deal of comfort. "I can hardly bear this, Uncle."

His uncle gave him a grim smile. "I'm afraid there is nothing more you can do, Henry."

Closing his eyes for a second or two, Henry drew in a deep breath, filling his lungs with sea air. How much he had changed in these last few months! How much he had grown! Jacintha was the only one he thought of, the only one in his heart. His affection for her, his love for her, was growing steadily until he thought it might burst from his chest.

"Very well," he muttered, turning his head to look at his uncle. "Then show me what I can do to help. I want to do all I can to stop Lord Slate."

CHAPTER SEVENTEEN

*J*acintha turned away from the window, her heart tumbling into her toes. Henry had been here and had been turned away. It was quite purposeful on Lord Slate's part, she was sure of that, although she was not sure as to why he might have done it. Was it in an attempt to keep her here, in the hope that she would give in to his demands to warm his bed before their supposed marriage. Not that she had any intention of marrying him, of course, for she was still determined that as soon as her father had recovered, they would leave this place.

Thankfully, her father was now doing much better than he had been two days ago, although she had not yet confessed the truth to him about what Lord Slate had done. Harmonia had accompanied her to dinner each evening and Lord Slate had been rather tight-lipped which had sent equal jolts of fear and relief straight through her. It was as though he could not say anything to her when Harmonia was present and, given that her sister insisted on accompanying her to her room once they retired, Lord Slate had very little opportunity to speak to her alone. Of course, Jacintha did not have anything in particular to say to him, finding herself shying away from him whenever she could.

If only she had seen Henry approach, then she might have made her way down below stairs in order to speak to him herself, but she had not been alerted to his presence until she had seen him from the window.

How much her heart had lifted at that moment, so glad to see him that tears had pricked at her eyes. They had then fallen like rain on her cheeks as he had ridden away, filled with sorrow that he had been forced to leave the estate. She had been filled with the urge to run after him, to beg him to help them escape from Lord Slate's home, but she had been forced to remain where she was, knowing that any attempt to do so would be prevented by either Lord Slate or his staff.

In the days she had been here, Jacintha had learned that Lord Slate's staff were particularly loyal to him. Her movements around the house had been noted and Lord Slate had told her, very firmly, that such explorations were not permitted. She had not returned to the library or the secret passage since, although she had wondered why he had appeared so concerned over her exploration of the house. Not that she had wanted to ask him, given his demeanor.

"We should prepare for dinner."

Turning to see Harmonia enter the room, Jacintha gave her a small smile. "I do not particularly wish to."

"I know, but we have very little choice," Harmonia replied, coming over to her and wrapping an arm around her shoulders. "Mayhap we should try to talk to Lord Slate a little more, in case that makes it easier. Mayhap he is feeling embarrassed and does not quite know how to smooth things over. Not that I am suggesting that you consider him again, for I certainly would not encourage you in that, but even some conversation might make things a little more amiable?"

Jacintha shook her head. "You are very good to try and think the best of people, Harmonia, but I cannot believe it."

Harmonia sighed. "I am sorry to hear it. However, you can draw comfort that the time here will be over soon. Papa will be ready to travel in a couple of days."

Jacintha's throat ached for a moment as she struggled to contain the tears that threatened to pour from her eyes. "Henry is here," she managed to say, looking over at her sister. "Lord Slate would not permit him to visit with us."

Harmonia's eyes widened in astonishment. "My goodness," she breathed. "Well, mayhap he will be able to accompany us when we return to London – or home, whichever father wishes."

"I wish he could help us," Jacintha whispered, a single tear falling from her eyes. "Oh, Harmonia, I have made such a mistake."

"Do not think about that now," Harmonia replied, firmly. "You must be strong for a little while longer, Jacintha. Just until papa is better. Then it will all be over."

Dinner was a tense affair. Lord Slate said very little, as usual, although his gaze remained fixed on Jacintha. Harmonia and Jacintha ate quickly, knowing that taking their time would not bring them any kind of reprieve.

"You have not gone exploring any more, have you?"

Jacintha looked up, trying to smile. "Of course not. I have been caught up with my father's wellbeing."

He grunted, looking rather relieved. "Good."

"Although I have been wondering about that passageway in the library," Harmonia interrupted, trying to smile at Lord Slate as though continuing the conversation was a good thing. "Where does it lead? Our own home has a few passages very similar to yours, although it simply leads to a different part of the house."

Jacintha groaned inwardly, aware of what Harmonia was trying to do but wishing that she had told Harmonia not to speak of the passageway to Lord Slate, worried that it would only make him angrier with her exploration of his home.

"The passageway?" Lord Slate repeated, a dark look appearing on his face. "When did you discover this?"

"Quite by accident, I assure you," Jacintha replied quickly, reaching under the table to squeeze Harmonia's hand so that she wouldn't say any more. "I closed the door at once when I realized what I had discovered. It is rather interesting, of course, but I would not want to pry."

He grunted, eyeing her with suspicion.

Lifting her chin, Jacintha returned his fierce gaze with one of her own. She was not about to be intimidated and Lord Slate's ferocious demeanor was not going to quell her spirit and she certainly would not apologize for stumbling across something quite unexpectedly. Nothing would induce her to do as he wished, no matter how angry he appeared.

"I saw Lord Musgrove came to call upon you today," she said, not quite sure where this sudden swell of bravery had come from. "What a shame that you could not admit him. I would have liked to greet him."

His brows lowered, his gaze narrowed.

"After all, he is a good friend of ours and I am delighted to know that he is nearby," she continued, hearing Harmonia's swift intake of breath. "I think his uncle lives nearby. Do you know him?"

"No, I do not," Lord Slate replied, tautly. He did not say any more but turned to his glass of port, refilling it almost to the brim and drinking from it heavily. Jacintha felt her stomach turn over but refused to allow any kind of fear to show in her expression. Seeing that Harmonia was close to finishing her own plate, Jacintha cleared her throat and settled her hands in her lap.

"I do hope you will not mind if we excuse ourselves to take tea in our room instead of in here," she said, calmly, looking over at the maid who bobbed a curtsy at once and left the room. "We need to ensure that Papa is sleeping well before we retire."

"Although I do hope that he will be up and about tomorrow," Harmonia added, making to rise from the table. "Do excuse us, Lord Slate, and thank you for an excellent dinner."

He shot to his feet, his hand shaking as he pointed one finger at Jacintha. "*You* will stay. Harmonia, you will go."

Harmonia caught Jacintha's hand, suddenly frozen in place.

"I don't think so, Lord Slate. That would be quite inappropriate," Jacintha said, as firmly as she could. "Do excuse us."

He stormed around the table, stopping just in front of them both. "There is something I wish to ask you in private, Jacintha. Your sister need not remain for this."

Jacintha swallowed hard, worried what he might do to Harmonia if she insisted that her sister remain.

"Very well, Lord Slate," she replied, hearing Harmonia's whispered "No, Jacintha!" coming from behind her.

Turning around to her sister, she gave Harmonia a tight smile. "I will be out in just a moment. Will you wait for me by the staircase?"

Harmonia did not answer her for a moment, her eyes wide with fear.

"Please, Harmonia," Jacintha urged, quietly. "I will be quite all right." She did not want to pretend that she was not scared of what Lord Slate intended, but nor did she want her sister to come to any harm. It was clear that Lord Slate was fueled both by anger and by liquor but Jacintha was determined that she would fight off any kind of advance. If she had to, she would scream aloud and Harmonia would be by her side in an instant.

"I warn you now, Lord Slate, that my father will know of all that passes between us," she said, calmly, as Harmonia reluctantly left the room, leaving the door wide open. "You tried to press your advances on me once before and I will not allow it to happen again."

"Of course not," he replied, although the dark look did not disappear from his face. "But what I have to ask you should be only between the two of us."

Jacintha looked up at him steadily with a confidence she did not feel. "If you are about to ask me to marry you, Lord Slate, I fear that you will be sadly disappointed."

His lip curled, his eyes narrowing. "Why would you refuse me?"

She shook her head, dampening down her anxiety in order to remain steadfast. "Are you truly asking me such a thing after how you have behaved?"

"I expect my wife to do as I ask – and not to go prying into things that do not concern her."

"Then I hope you find a wife who is willing to do as you ask," Jacintha replied, making for the door. "Do excuse me, Lord Slate. I have the feeling that we will be leaving your home within the next few days."

He lurched for the door, slamming it hard before she could reach it.

"You have seen too much," he snarled, grasping her shoulder. "I cannot allow you to leave me. You *will* marry me, Jacintha, or it will be all the worse for you."

A curling fear made her wrench herself away from him, wondering what it was he meant. "I have seen nothing, Lord Slate," she said, moving around the table so as to put something in between them. "You are talking nonsense."

"You should never have snooped around my home," he said, slamming one fist down on the table. "You should have kept your nose out of my business!"

Without having the smallest idea of what he was talking about, Jacintha stared at him in confusion. "Lord Slate, I will not be marrying you. I have no idea of what it is you are speaking, and I intend to leave this house at the soonest opportunity."

Letting out a roar of frustration, Lord Slate made to race around the table towards her, only for Harmonia to open the door, her eyes wide and face pale. Jacintha darted for the door, pulling it firmly behind her before rushing Harmonia up the stairs to her room, her heart beating wildly in her chest.

"You must sleep in my room tonight," Harmonia exclaimed, as they reached her bedchamber and, with as much haste as they could manage, shut the door behind them before locking it securely. "I will not allow you to sleep in a room alone. He has keys to the house, Jacintha!"

"I think it best," Jacintha replied, her hand over her frantically beating heart. "Goodness, Harmonia, thank you for coming when you did. I do not know what would have happened should he have reached me." She shuddered, still feeling panic swirling around her. "He thinks I have seen something I ought not to and insists that I marry him so that he can keep my neck in a noose."

"You *know* papa will not have it. We will be quite safe here together, I am sure of it."

Jacintha shook her head. "We will need to push something heavy in front of the door before I can sleep a wink."

Together, they shoved a heavy set of drawers against the door, both of them breathing hard as they pushed it into place. Sagging against the wall for a moment, Jacintha closed her eyes and thought of Henry. He was nearby, close to them all and that in itself was a comfort. If only he had been able to come into the house today, then she would have been able to tell him just how sorry she was for ignoring her heart and thinking only of practicality. Would she ever get another chance to explain to him where she had gone wrong?

"It is done," Harmonia said quietly, taking Jacintha's hand and leading her to the table and chairs by the fire, where a tea tray sat waiting for them. "Come now, you need to rest. We both do. Everything will change come the morrow. I know we will be gone from this place as soon as papa is recovered."

CHAPTER EIGHTEEN

*M*uch to her surprise, Jacintha slept well that night, probably because she had her sister next to her and the chest of drawers against the door. Her exhausted mind had refused to dream and so she slept soundly, only to wake the following morning with a deep sense of foreboding.

The banging at the door alerted her to the fact that the maids were trying to get in with Harmonia's breakfast tray. Rousing her sister, they stumbled, bleary eyed, towards the door and moved the chest of drawers back into its original position before unlocking the door.

Grateful it was their own maid who appeared at the door, Jacintha gave her swift instructions to have her breakfast tray brought to Harmonia's room, as well as a change of clothes. The maid was dispatched quickly and, ensuring that the door was locked and the key left in the door, Harmonia and Jacintha sat down, placing their chairs directly in the stream of sunshine coming from the window

"At least it cheers the spirit," Jacintha murmured, softly.

"I *must* speak to papa this morning, even if he is not ready to rise from his bed."

"I think he will be ready," Harmonia replied, encouragingly. "He was in good spirits yesterday."

Jacintha nodded, remembering how her father had smiled up at her from his bed, the color back in his cheeks. "I just hope this news will not throw him back into weakness."

"I doubt it," Harmonia replied, with a quick smile. "I think it will put a fire into his bones, pushing him to leave this house at once." She put a gentle hand on Jacintha's arm. "You know he will believe every word you say."

Thankfully, two hours later, Jacintha found that Harmonia had been right. Her father was in a blaze of fury on hearing what had occurred, enraged that Lord Slate had tried such things with his daughter. He exclaimed over how respectable Lord Slate had appeared, how trustworthy and honest, only for him to try and take advantage of Jacintha when she had been entrusted to his care.

"We shall pack immediately," he declared, getting up from his chair and ringing the bell so furiously that Jacintha thought he might pull it from the rafters. "And where is the man? I wish to speak to him before we depart."

"He – he has gone out on business, my lord," the Duke's manservant replied, emerging from the shadows in order to begin preparations to leave. "I do not know when he will return."

"You will not call him out, papa," Jacintha said, firmly, appreciating her father's anger for her sake, but not wishing him to be hurt. "I am quite safe, as you can see. You do not need to involve swords or the like."

Her father shook his head, his lip curling. "I would very much like to inflict some kind of injury on that man, but I will not," he said, decisively. "I know all too well that he has more youth and strength on his side, but I *will* ensure that all of society knows of his behavior. I will not allow him to continue with his good name intact."

Jacintha left him then, glad that all seemed to be at an end. They would leave Ferryway and return home where she might forget entirely about Lord Slate – and think only of Henry. How much she wished to see him! Especially when she could tell him just how much of a comfort he had been to her, even through the window of Lord Slate's home.

Walking back to her bedchamber, Jacintha drew in a great breath, relieved that the entire experience was coming to an end. She had no need to worry any longer. Lord Slate would soon be nothing more than a distant memory.

"There you are!"

Jacintha let out a frightened squeak as Lord Slate slammed one hand over her mouth, his other hand grasping her arm tightly. His damp clothes pressed against hers, making her shiver.

"I knew you'd come back here eventually," he hissed, pushing the door shut with his body and letting go of her mouth. "I told you that you've already seen too much. You're going to be my wife whether you like it or not."

"What do you think you are doing?" Jacintha gasped, struggling to get away from him. "I haven't seen anything. Please, let me go."

He chuckled darkly, his eyes narrowing as he dragged her towards the other side of her bedchamber. For a moment, Jacintha thought he meant to ruin her, tugging away from him all the more, but, much to her astonishment, he pushed aside the large tapestry that had been draped on the wall and, after another moment of searching, pulled open a door.

"You spoke to your father, I presume," he spat, wrestling her through the door and pushing her in front of him. "I heard that various arrangements had been made for your departure."

Panic was swirling through her so strongly that Jacintha couldn't think what to do or what to say. Her limbs became wooden, Lord Slate's rough hands the only thing forcing her to keep moving.

"I told you I would not allow it," Lord Slate continued, his voice echoing through the tunnel as they began to descend some stone steps. "I mean what I say, Jacintha."

"My father will not stand for this," Jacintha managed to say, her fingernails scraping on the stone walls as she struggled to make her way down without falling. There were a few lit candles on the walls but that gave her very little light to see by. She had no idea what Lord Slate had planned for her, nor what it was he was so frightened of her revealing to others. "You know that he will come after you."

"He will be powerless, given that you will be my wife by that time," Lord Slate replied, darkly. "Do not think you can escape from me this time, Jacintha. I will have you."

Her breath was coming so fast she thought she might faint from the fear of what Lord Slate intended for her, the realization that no one - neither Harmonia, her father or Henry - knew where she was or what was happening to her. They had all assumed that Lord Slate had gone from the estate, but it was clear that he had used these secret passages to return without anyone being aware of his presence.

"Where are we going?" she whispered, seeing the floor

become level once more with another wooden door just ahead of them.

"The trapdoor, my dear," he replied, sounding surprised that she had not yet worked it out. "That door you found, the one you told your sister about, I am sure you saw the trapdoor there and wondered what it was for."

"I did not question it," Jacintha lied, even though she knew such a thing would not change his mind. "I have had no thought of it since."

He snorted, reaching past her to open the door before hurrying her through it. "You are not a particularly good liar, Jacintha. Now hurry up and move along. The trapdoor is just ahead of you and you will find it already open for you. All your burning questions will be answered in one moment."

Jacintha turned her head and saw the door to the library and, in a moment of panic, rushed for it – only to discover that it did not open for her. Lord Slate grasped her arm and tugged her away, jarring her arm.

"You little brat," he snarled, dragging her so close to him that she was forced to look up into his face. "When will you learn that you can't escape from me? I'll do whatever I must in order to get you to submit. Now get down that ladder and don't try such a thing again, or it will be all the worse for you."

All the strength left her body, weakness rifling through her. She was trapped, tied to Lord Slate forever unless she could find a way to get away from him. The walls seemed to close in around her, the air becoming thick.

"Now don't try that on me," Lord Slate murmured, a warning tone settling over his voice. "Who knows what I might have to do to you in order to revive you?" His hand trailed down over her arm, down the curve of her waist and beyond. "Do I make myself clear?"

Shuddering at his touch, Jacintha nodded and began to move away from him towards the trapdoor. Screaming would do no good, the walls were too thick to alert anyone – and even his staff, should they hear her, would most likely ignore her cries for help.

She had no choice. Peering down at the trapdoor and seeing the rope ladder swinging from it, she began to gingerly climb down. Lord Slate grasped her arms roughly, ensuring that she would not slip, and Jacintha descended further into the gloom until another pair of hands caught her.

Shrieking aloud earned her nothing more than a hard slap, the shock of it stunning her into silence.

"Careful, there," Lord Slate said angrily, as he came to join Jacintha and the other man. "She belongs to me and no-one else. Understand?"

"Understood, my lord," came the gruff reply. "Now, are you sure you're not wanting to wait here for a time? The boat is a little around the mainland so it is out of sight of the shore, but it's still awful risky."

"I don't have a choice," Lord Slate grated, tugging Jacintha along as he began to make his way down the cold stone floor of the tunnel. "Her father would have taken her away and I couldn't let her go. She knows too much."

"I don't know anything," Jacintha cried, her heart crying out in fear. "I don't know a thing about this place or what you're doing."

The man who had caught her as she descended laughed harshly. "Of course you'd say anything to get away, wouldn't you? Pretending you don't know about the smuggling."

Jacintha looked over at him, the lantern he held casting

strange, murky shadows across his face. "What are you talking about?"

The man chuckled, his eyes dark. "Do you not know by now? Your Lord Slate here is a smuggler."

"A – a smuggler?" Jacintha stammered, hardly able to believe it.

"One of the best," the man replied, as the first shards of daylight began to pierce the tunnel's darkness. "And soon you'll be joining the operation, I've no doubt about it."

"That she will," Lord Slate replied, his voice echoing around the tunnel walls. "She won't have a choice."

Jacintha continued to stumble down the tunnel, hearing the sound of lapping water from below. The crash of the waves only added to her fright, her hand tightening on Lord Slate's sleeve as he held her arm. She hated having to lean on him but, given the circumstances, she had very little choice.

"The boat's below, my lord," the other man said, as they came near to what appeared to be a large hole in the tunnel floor. "Stevenson's waiting."

"Very good," Lord Slate grated, giving Jacintha a slight shove. "Now, climb down there and don't dare make a sound."

Seeing the other smuggler sit down on the edge of the hole before climbing down what appeared to be another rope ladder, Jacintha had no other choice but to follow suit, her dress growing damp and clammy around her legs. Her legs trembled as she tried to make her way down the ladder, only for hands to grab at her feet, making her shriek aloud.

"Quiet!" Lord Slate exclaimed from above her. "I said not a sound."

Jacintha shuddered violently as she was helped to a small boat, not able to so much as look at the two men who had helped her into the boat. They were in a large cave with only a small opening between themselves and the open sea.

"Quickly, my lord," one of the smugglers called, as Lord Slate descended. "The tide is against us."

Jacintha watched as Lord Slate climbed into the boat, before wrapping up the rope ladder and tying it securely with a smaller piece of rope. It dangled there, almost invisible to the naked eye, and certainly not easily spotted unless you knew it was there.

"On we go," Lord Slate instructed, as he took his seat. "And be on your guard. I am not certain that this next part will go as smoothly as we had hoped."

As the boat left the cave, Jacintha blinked furiously as she looked up into the blue sky, wondering if this would be the last time she would see England's shores. Turning her head to look over at the beach, she thought for a moment about jumping into the sea, trying her best to swim to the shore, only to realize that she would be dragged to the bottom in seconds. Her skirts would fill with water and, given that she was already feeling rather weak, she knew she wouldn't have the strength to even attempt to get to shore. Feeling desperate, she looked over at the shore with grief growing in her heart, seeing a small figure on horseback racing across the shoreline. She could hear nothing but the sound of the waves and the cries of the gulls as they circled overhead. Any remaining hope that she might escape flickered and died, quenched by the anguish she felt. She would never see her sisters again, never see her father. Henry would be nothing more than a memory.

There was nothing but darkness waiting for her.

CHAPTER NINETEEN

*A*fter they had been turned away from Lord Slate's home, Henry had not stopped thinking of Jacintha. Even though he had been a part of the discussion over what the men had discovered in the caves, they could not exactly mount an attack on Lord Slate's home without finding evidence of the supposed contraband. There had to be a way to link Lord Slate to the smuggling, otherwise, their entire operation would be utterly useless. Yes, they had one smuggler in custody but that meant nothing if they couldn't catch Lord Slate. Were he to get away with what he had done, then Henry would be more than angry, especially if he still had Jacintha by his side. A man ought to pay for his crimes.

Even though his uncle had insisted that he rest before going out on patrol in the hope the smugglers might place more contraband in Lord Slate's tunnel, Henry had tossed and turned, his mind caught up with thoughts of Jacintha. He had walked under the stars, looking over at the manor house and wondering if the flickering lights within came from her room. Was she safe? Was she still as sure about Lord Slate as she had been before? Over and over, he had cursed his lack of clarity when he had been in London. If only he had seen her for what she was back then, if only he had stopped himself from becoming the cad and the rogue he had been, then things might have worked out very differently.

"Here."

Looking up from where he sat, Henry saw his uncle standing beside him, handing him a roll filled with something that smelled delicious.

"One of the men is a baker," Roderick explained, coming to sit down beside Henry, who was leaning heavily against a tree trunk. "He saw that you've been out for most of the night and didn't intend to go home."

"I need to watch the house," Henry muttered, rubbing his eyes. "I can't let Lord Slate get away with this."

Roderick let out a long sigh. "The men didn't find anything."

"Nothing?"

He shook his head. "No, nothing. The tunnel was empty."

"So we have no proof," Henry muttered, before biting into the roll, his stomach growling appreciatively.

Roderick sighed heavily. "Nothing yet. But we will. Eventually. There are men on patrol day and night, even though you might not always see them."

"Getting Lord Slate eventually isn't good enough," Henry replied at once, gesturing towards the manor house. "I cannot wait around for him to allow me to see Jacintha! She might be in danger."

"I agree," Roderick replied, heavily. "However, short of barging in and demanding to see her, which would only alert him to how close we are to catching him, I think the only thing we can do is wait."

Henry's lip curled, his jaw clenching. "I don't like it, Uncle."

"I can tell," Roderick replied, his words tainted with good humor. "But she is there with her sister and her father, what could Lord Slate possibly do to her under those circumstances?"

Shrugging, Henry finished the last of his roll, thinking hard. "I'm not sure, uncle. I don't want to speculate but I get the feeling that all is not well with Jacintha under his roof."

There was a short silence, with both pairs of eyes looking over at the manor house, the sound of the ocean waves lapping at the shore the only sound.

"Well, at least you're well-hidden here," Roderick replied, getting to his feet and gesturing to the tree Henry was sitting under, which was surrounded by the tall waving beach grasses. "If I hadn't known you were sitting here then I wouldn't have seen you."

"Good," Henry muttered, his gaze narrowing as he saw some movement at the manor house. "That is just what I was hoping for."

"Are you going to sit out here all day?"

"If I have to," Henry said, firmly. "I'll be along to the house if I see anything."

"Very good," Roderick replied, with a quick smile. "Try not to worry too much, Henry. And, if you see anything, for heaven's sake don't take it on yourself!"

Henry nodded, watching his uncle walk away before returning his gaze to the manor house. Whilst he did want to watch what was going on at the house, his ultimate goal was Jacintha. If Lord Slate left, then he would simply make his way to the house to call on her, even without Lord Slate's permission to enter his home.

He wasn't quite sure how long he sat there, glad that the sun was already warming his chilled bones. The night had been cool, with the sea air adding to the chill. Now, at least, he was warm and not as hungry as he had been before.

A sudden movement caught his eye, making him sit up straight. A horse was making its way from the manor house towards the gate and Henry was sure he knew who it was.

It could only be Lord Slate.

The man was riding at a gallop, coming out towards the shore. Henry held his breath, remaining exactly where he was. He wondered if Lord Slate might make his way towards the caves, only to realize that the man would not be that stupid nor that obvious. Besides, the tide had turned some time ago, which meant that some of the caves would not be accessible in anything other than a boat very soon.

Watching closely, Henry saw Lord Slate take a turn up towards the village, his horse's hooves digging into the sand. Torn between a desire to follow him and to find Jacintha, he paused for a moment before getting to his feet, knowing that he needed to talk to Jacintha. His uncle could deal with Lord Slate and he was sure there were other men watching, just like his uncle had said.

Wishing he had thought to bring a horse, Henry tramped his way towards Slate's home, his heart thundering wildly as he thought about Jacintha. She *would* be willing to see him, would she not? He couldn't bear it if she had turned her back on him now, aligning herself with Lord Slate.

Then he remembered how she had looked at him

through the window and hope burst to life within his heart. She was waiting for him, wanted to speak to him. He had to believe it.

"Open up!"

Henry thundered on the door, his hand beginning to pain him as he banged on it again and again.

No-one answered.

He had been knocking on the door for a good few minutes now and still, no-one came to answer him. He had no idea where Lord Slate's staff had gone, wondering whether or not Jacintha and her family still remained inside or if they had left without his knowledge. Surely they could not have returned to London without him seeing, given that he had watched the house all day? His heart began to thud wildly in his chest, anxiety rising with every breath he took.

"Henry?"

"Jacintha?" he shouted, as the door handle turned underneath his hand. "Is that you?"

It was none other than Harmonia who stood there, her eyes wide and cheeks pale. "Henry! Whatever is the matter?"

"Jacintha," he said, stepping inside. "Where is she?"

"I – I don't know," Harmonia replied, looking about rather helplessly. "I don't even know where the staff has gone. I heard you knocking and tried to ring for the butler or the maid but no-one came. What is going on?"

Henry grasped her hands, seeing her white face. "Is your father here?"

"He has been unwell almost since the day we arrived," Harmonia replied, shivering just a little. "Lord Slate has been....he has not treated Jacintha well, Henry. I am afraid of him, just as she is. He is not the man we thought."

"I know that," Henry said, firmly, trying not to let his own concern show. "Now listen, Harmonia, where is Jacintha? We must find her and prepare to leave this place at once."

"We have been packing," Harmonia replied, hurrying towards the staircase and gesturing for him to follow. "Jacintha told father everything this morning and, given that he is now well enough to travel, we were to leave as soon as possible."

"Then we must fetch her," Henry replied at once, filled with a deep sense of happiness that Jacintha was not to wed Lord Slate. "I must know that she is well. There is more to Lord Slate than even she knows."

Harmonia knocked on the door of the bedchamber before turning the handle and stepping inside – only to stop dead. Henry, forced to step back in order not to bump into her, tried to look past her shoulder.

"She's not here," Harmonia whispered, turning around slowly to face him. "I – I don't know where she would have gone."

"Would she be somewhere else in the house?" Henry asked, a slow rising panic growing in his chest. "Is there anywhere else she might have gone?"

Harmonia shook her head, her eyes wide with fright. "No, she was afraid of Lord Slate and even though we knew he had gone, Jacintha was determined to stay in her room with the door locked. She wanted to ensure her packing was going smoothly."

Henry put his hand on the doorframe to steady himself, his mind scrambling to think of where Jacintha might be.

"I saw Lord Slate leaving," he said, looking over at

Harmonia. "Do you know where he went? Has he returned?"

A deep sense of foreboding filled him as Harmonia shook her head, her hands clutching his arm. The fact that Lord Slate's staff appeared to be entirely absent only added to his concern.

"Go and care for your father," he said, trying to smile at her. "You need not worry. I will find Jacintha. Do not tell your father if you think it will only make him worse. Resume your packing. Once I return with her, I shall take you all to my uncle's home. Trust me, Harmonia. I will return with her."

She nodded, her eyes wide and filled with fright. "Thank you, Henry," she whispered, clearly struggling to keep her composure. "Godspeed."

He hated leaving her when she appeared so pale and wane, but having no other choice, he clattered down the stairs and raced back outside, running to the stables to find a horse. Within minutes, he was riding flat out across the sands, coming to a sudden stop when his uncle appeared at the other end of the beach, waving to him frantically.

"Where have you been?" his uncle demanded, as Henry jumped down from his horse. "I've been looking for you!"

"Lord Slate left so I went in search of Jacintha," Henry gasped, his heart racing. "Why? What's happened?"

"One of the men came to find me," his uncle replied, glancing behind him as some men rushed past towards the shore. "They saw a figure walk out into the waves towards a small boat with two men in it. They picked him up before heading towards the caves."

"The cave with the tunnel?" Henry asked, his body growing taut with tension.

"Yes, the very one," his uncle replied. "There are two

boats being prepared. One of the scouts informed me that there is a larger ship waiting around the headland." He paused and put one hand on Henry's arm. "Only a few minutes ago, we saw that boat leaving the cave – just as you rode towards us. They had one more person on board than when they entered."

Henry looked at his uncle, a slow dawning realization coming over him. "You think that extra person is Jacintha."

"I do," his uncle replied, leading him towards the shoreline. "Hurry now. The boats are being prepared."

Henry felt sick to his stomach, a knot of fear tightening in his gut. Lord Slate had taken Jacintha through the tunnel and onto the boat, evidently determined to marry her whatever it took. He couldn't think of what to do, the anger he felt over Lord Slate's cruelty making his hands curl slowly into fists.

Looking out across the sea, he saw the boat moving away from them, urgency filling him.

"Quickly now!" he called, springing into action and hurrying towards the boats. "We cannot lose them!"

"And we won't," his uncle assured him, stepping into one of the boats and gesturing for Henry to climb into the other. "Don't worry, Henry. This all comes to an end today."

The boat rocked on the waves and, as the other men climbed aboard, Henry grasped the oars firmly, pulling them through the water with as much strength as he could muster. The oars dug deeply into the water and, within a few minutes, they were away from the beach and heading towards the ship. Henry twisted his head around to see the smaller boat already beside the larger ship, hearing the sound of faint shouts coming across the waves.

He couldn't lose her, not when he was so close. If that

ship made headway, then they'd never catch it. Despite his uncle's promises, Henry knew that there was a chance Lord Slate might just slip through their fingers. They *had* to reach the ship before it weighed anchor. He had to get to Jacintha in time.

CHAPTER TWENTY

*J*acintha shivered violently as she was hauled up onto the ship, finding herself almost too weak to stand. All around her stood men of different ages, each leering at her as they laughed at her terrified expression.

"Leave her be," Lord Slate shouted, as he climbed aboard just behind her. "She's mine, understand? No-one else is to touch her." Grasping her arm roughly, he gave Jacintha a slight shake, pointing at each of the men. "I'll have you thrown overboard if you so much as lay a finger on her."

A little relieved that she would, at least, be protected from that, Jacintha let out a long, shaky breath, her eyes lifting just a little to look out over the horizon. There were boats in the distance, but she supposed they were just more of Lord Slate's men. Clearly, she hadn't known this man at all. He had been leading an entirely different life, one she hadn't even known about.

"We need to go, Captain," Lord Slate stated, firmly, as

the last of the men climbed aboard. "I'll be taking her to my cabin. Weigh anchor."

The captain stepped forward and nodded, shouting out orders which sent the men scrambling across the deck at once. Jacintha had no choice but to follow him, her heart pounding with fright as Lord Slate dragged her across the deck and down some small wooden steps into what she presumed to be his cabin. With a hard shove, she stumbled inside, only for him to slam the door hard, although he did not lock it.

Jacintha tried to get her bearing, looking all around the large cabin and finding that there was nowhere for her to hide. There was a large bed on one side, and a table and chairs at the other, with only a few other pieces of furniture.

"You're not going anywhere, Jacintha, so you can stop trying to find a place to hide yourself," Lord Slate chuckled, as he threw his coat over the back of one of the chairs. "You're going to have to learn how to be my wife, although I'm happy to teach you all you need to know."

The gleam in his eyes made her shudder, moving away from him to put the table and chairs in between them both.

"Come now, Jacintha," Lord Slate said lazily, as though he knew she would have to give in to him eventually. "This isn't going to work. There's nowhere for you to go. I'm the only friend you have in the world now."

"Why are you doing this?" Jacintha asked, hoarsely. "What have I ever done to you to deserve this?"

He shrugged, sitting down on the bed and studying her. "You seemed perfectly eligible," he replied, calmly, as though discussing the weather and not her kidnapping. "I needed a wife, you see. The heir and all that."

"But you didn't want me to know who you really were,"

Jacintha interrupted, clinging onto the back of a chair for dear life. "You didn't want to tell me the truth."

His eyes darkened and his lips flattened into an angry line.

"Did you really think that once I came here, I would be induced to marry you?" Jacintha continued, her words becoming a little stronger as she spoke, attempting to gather some courage.

Lord Slate snorted. "You were never meant to come here until we were wed," he exclaimed, pointing at her. "It was you that made this happen! You told me your father was thinking of returning to the country so how else was I to get you here? Whether you were induced or forced to marry me, I did not particularly care...as you see."

"But why?" Jacintha asked, feeling almost numb with fear and cold. "Why did you choose me? I am sure there are plenty of other eligible women who would have very little concern for your behavior, who would overlook it."

He shook his head, a grim smile playing around his mouth. "Because I have already made more than enough of an effort to claim you as my bride. I will not do so again."

Jacintha sagged against the chair, hot tears burning in her eyes although she refused to let them fall. "So that is what I am to you, is it? Nothing more than a project."

"I needed a wife, Jacintha. I chose you. That means I expect to have you. I will not go back to London and repeat the process all over again. It is simply not worth it. Not when I have you. Besides, even if I had thought to let you go, I could not have done so, given that you sneaked through my house and discovered the tunnel."

"Please," Jacintha replied, desperately, knowing that her explanation was more than useless at this point and yet finding words tumbling from her mouth. "I tried to find the library and came upon it by accident. I had no idea of any of this!" she finished, gesturing to the ship. "I don't even understand what it is you are involved in!"

"Don't be so ridiculous," Lord Slate growled, his eyes narrowing. "I know your sharp mind. You can try and play the fool all you like but I know you worked it out – and even if you did not realize it at the time, you would have told someone eventually."

"So you are a smuggler, then?" Jacintha asked, a faint stirring of anger amongst her fear and confusion. "Why do it, Lord Slate? Why bother when you are already a wealthy man?"

"Because one can never have too much wealth," he replied, with a dark glint in his eye. "And because, once I discovered the tunnel in the old place, it seemed foolish not to get a share of what was being brought in."

"You are meant to be a pillar of society," Jacintha retorted, angry with herself over how easily she had been duped by him. "You are meant to be upstanding, an example to the rest of us – and yet you engage in such illegal activities as this?" She did not mean to anger him, did not mean to upset him when she was in such a precarious situation but her frustrations and confusion tore from her lips, desperate to know who Lord Slate truly was.

He got to his feet, striding towards her and, much to her fright, threw himself over the table and grabbed her arm as one chair fell, crashing, to the floor.

"Don't start getting yourself all high and mighty with me, Jacintha," he spat, his fingers digging cruelly into the soft skin of her arms. "This is a very different world you've come into now and if there's one thing you need to learn, it's not to question me. *Never* question me."

She looked back at him, her eyes burning into his as she

battled with the fear that was racing all through her. She did not want to simply curl up and give in, even if she was about to set sail for an entirely different land, an entirely new world. Lord Slate was not going to have a quiet and obedient little wife. She would endure what she had to, in order to make him as miserable as she could.

There would be pain and suffering, but she would not shirk from it.

His mouth landed on hers and Jacintha felt her courage die almost immediately as she tried to fight him off, realizing that his strength was simply too much for her. Her gown tore, his hands scrabbling at the neckline of her gown, but Jacintha did not give up.

Lifting her knee high, she rammed it hard into him, only for him to stagger back with a howl of pain. She darted away from him, seeing the anger in his eyes as he struggled to breathe enough to shout for help.

The door handle slipped under her fingers. Jacintha did not know what she was doing, for to leave the cabin now would leave her to face a group of hostile smugglers, but everything was screaming at her to get away from Lord Slate however she could. Her heart beating wildly, she opened the door – only to see men climbing over the rail of the ship. There were wild shouts and harsh cries – but Jacintha did not wait. There were some steps to her left, steps that led deeper into the body of the ship, and Jacintha hurried down them at once. Three other men ran past her but none of them seemed to notice her. The shouts and clash of swords caught her ears as she made her way below deck, her fright rising steadily.

Turning this way and that, Jacintha tried to find somewhere that could hide her. If there had been any way to jump out into the sea, with something she could hold onto to help her float, she would do it in a moment but everywhere she looked, all she could see was gloomy darkness.

The air was stale, the smell penetrating her nose and making her stomach roll with nausea. She found the kitchens, complete with the cook who glared at her and started towards her, only for her to scurry away in fright. The shouts and cries of the men above her filled her with fear, worried that she was caught in the middle of some kind of smuggler attack. If they found her, would she be taken away as a prize for the victor? Would she be seen as nothing more than merchandise, sold to the highest bidder? Would there be a ransom sent to her father in exchange for her life?

Shivering violently, Jacintha continued to search the ship, knowing that her search would, ultimately, be hopeless. She would hide for a time but Lord Slate would find her eventually. There was no escaping from him.

Weakness filled her limbs as she continued to search, eventually coming across a room with a small, sputtering lantern on one wall and a small porthole window at the other.

The small room was at the very back of the ship, filled with barrels and containers. Lifting the lid, Jacintha realized that this was where the food for the journey was stored. There was nowhere else to go but here, for she could not just keep searching until she was caught. Her body was tired. She needed to sit down.

At least there was ample space to hide without being seen and, given that she had few other options open to her, Jacintha scurried to the smallest, darkest corner she could find and sat down on the wooden floor.

No footsteps came after her, no-one called her name. For the time being, at least, she was given a slight reprieve.

The barrels and containers hid her well but, as she sat

there alone in the gloom, tears began to pour down her cheeks. Trying her best to keep her sobbing at bay, she buried her head in her hands and wept, feeling trapped and alone.

There was no-one here to save her. She had nowhere else to go but here. Lifting her head, she looked out of the porthole window and saw nothing but the sea. There was not even a glimpse of land. She was completely and utterly trapped.

Pounding feet above her made her cringe with fright, her heart beating so loudly she was certain it might give her away. Not that it mattered, she supposed for, in time she would either be caught or be forced to leave the quiet room in search of water.

"Oh, Henry," she murmured, leaning her head back against the wall and allowing her thoughts to turn towards him. "If only we had allowed that to happen," she whispered, thinking of that day all those years ago when he had held her so closely in the gardens. "What would have become of us now?"

Their future might have been so very different, their lives stayed on the same path instead of growing steadily more separate. She might never have convinced herself to choose a marriage of convenience instead of love, might have listened to her heart and chosen Henry over everyone else.

And now, it was much too late.

Would she ever see Harmonia and her father again? What about her other sisters and their children? She would become nothing more than a memory, a sad story told amongst family as they wondered where she was, desperately praying for her return. Jacintha did not even know if she would survive whatever it was Lord Slate had planned for her. His violence and temper left her in no doubt that he would use his strength in whatever way he wanted in order to get her to obey. She might be as strong and as resolute as she could but, in time, that determination would be broken. *She* would be broken.

Closing her eyes, Jacintha let tears fall down her cheeks, crying for what she had missed and for the family she would never see again. Her hope and courage flickered and died, shrouding her in darkness and defeat.

All hope was gone.

CHAPTER TWENTY-ONE

"*H*urry, men!" Roderick shouted, as the two boats surged forward towards the larger vessel. "We are almost upon them."

Henry felt as though his entire body was on fire, his limbs screaming in pain as he dug the oars into the water again and again. He could not stop, despite the agony, knowing that he *had* to reach Jacintha.

If they lost the ship now, then she would be gone forever.

"They are preparing to attack!" one man shouted, unsheathing his sword and moving to stand near the front of Henry's boat, his balance impeccable. "Get ready men."

Henry looked over at Roderick, seeing him take his boat around to the opposite side of the ship, so that they would divide the men onboard. Aware that he did not have his own sword with him, Henry was more than relieved when another man put a sheathed sword down over his knees, just as they drew level to the ship.

Henry was not quite sure how he managed to climb on board, such was the hubbub and the fray going on all around him. Somehow, the men with him managed to secure their small boat to the larger one and, with their swords in their hands, they climbed aboard, battling their way as they did so.

He was the second last to leave the boat, adrenaline rushing through his veins as he held his sword in one hand and carefully climbed his way up onto the deck.

A battle was raging all around him, the sounds of clashing swords and screams of pain filling his ears. From the other side of the deck, Henry saw his uncle fighting hard, his sword glinting in the sunshine.

A howl of rage caught his ears and, in a moment, Henry found himself in the middle of it all. Glad that he had endured years of training with the sword, Henry put into practice every last thing he had learned, managing to disarm more than one of his opponents. They fell in front of him, the rest of the men doing the same. He did not know how long he fought, sweat trickling down his back as he slashed wildly at two men who came to attack him at once.

And then, just behind them, he saw a glimmer of movement.

Anger burned in his veins as he saw Lord Slate was slowly making his way out of a cabin, his own sword in his hand. He was not fighting, nor was he making any attempt to join his smugglers in the fight. Did he have Jacintha inside? Where was she?

Another man fell in front of him and, turning his attention to the second, Henry quickly knocked him to the ground, leaving him to the rest of the men to deal with. The battle was slowly being won, and he was not about to let Lord Slate escape from what he had done. He saw the man hurry towards the side of the ship, realizing what he intended to do. Slate wanted to use one of the boats in an attempt to get away, to save his own hide.

The man had no courage.

With a shout of rage, Henry rushed forward, his sword held out towards Lord Slate. The man turned at once, his stance ready and prepared for Henry's attack.

Henry had always known that to fight with a clear mind brought the best possible outcome but now, he fought Lord Slate with all the fury he felt. His sword fell like hammer blows, clearly surprising Lord Slate, who struggled to hold Henry back. Lord Slate fell back against the ship, his sword thrown from his hand which landed with a harmless splash in the sea beneath.

"Oh no, you don't," Henry grated, grasping Lord Slate's collar with one hand, his eyes boring into his. "Don't even think of trying to escape. I will not allow it." He raised his sword and carefully pressed the cold steel against Lord Slate's neck – and, for the first time, he saw Lord Slate look afraid.

"You are the most conniving, cruel gentleman I have ever had the pleasure of knowing," Henry grated, resisting the urge to slice open Lord Slate's neck. "Now, where is she?"

Lord Slate made to shrug, only for Henry to shake him, hard. "Do not even think of lying to me, Lord Slate, or it will be all the worse for you."

The slight gleam in Lord Slate's eye faded, his whole body slumping in defeat.

"I don't know," he muttered, dropping his head. "She escaped from my cabin."

The words hit Henry like a sharp kick to his gut. "When?"

"Before you arrived," Lord Slate muttered, his voice a little hoarse as Henry tightened his grip on his neck. "I don't know where she's gone, I swear to you."

Henry had no choice but to believe him, closing his eyes for a moment in order to steady his breathing. Jacintha *had* to be on board, although what Lord Slate had done to her, he couldn't imagine.

"You are going to pay for your crimes," he breathed, opening his eyes to glare at Lord Slate. "Trust me when I tell you that there is no escape for you this time. You may be a man of the nobility but that will not protect you, not in this case. Your time is up, Lord Slate."

Holding his sword away from Lord Slate's neck, he dragged the man back towards his uncle and the rest of his men, relieved to see that the victory had been achieved.

"Throw them all in the brig," Roderick was commanding, as the men began to haul their captives towards the lower part of the ship. "Ah, Henry. Caught your man, have you?" Roderick's eyes glittered as he pointed his sword at Lord Slate, a small smile on his face. "I can't tell you how glad I am to see you, Lord Slate. We have a lovely little jail cell waiting for you back on land."

Lord Slate snarled, his eyes flashing. "I have nothing to say to you."

"That's quite all right," Roderick replied, cheerfully. "It's not me you're going to have to explain yourself to."

Taking Lord Slate by the arm, he nodded to Henry. "Go and find her. I'll take things from here."

Henry nodded and turned away at once, only one thing on his mind.

Finding Jacintha.

· · ·

Hurrying to the cabin, he began to look for her in every place he could find, calling her name as he did so. She had to be here somewhere, for she certainly would not have gone into the sea in an attempt to make it to land. He wasn't even sure she could swim!

Leaving Lord Slate's cabin, Henry began to search the Captain's cabin before heading below deck. The air was stale, the smell of unwashed bodies and old food mingling together to make a rather heady concoction. Struggling to see in the gloom, Henry began to call her name over and over, desperately hoping that she would recognize his voice.

"Jacintha? It's Henry. Come out, please!" His voice echoed around the ship, disappearing into all the dark nooks and crannies. "Jacintha? It's Henry."

There was no response. Fear began to tighten its noose around Henry's neck, making him terrified for her safety. What had Lord Slate done to her? He paused, one hand on the back of a chair as he leaned forward, drawing in long, slow breaths.

He had to find her. She had to be here.

"Henry?"

He looked up at once, his eyes piercing the gloom. A wraith stood in the doorway of a small room, a shadowy figure leaning heavily against the doorframe. His muscles weakened, his body sagging in relief.

"Jacintha?"

A soft cry came from her mouth as he stumbled towards her, clasping her tightly in his arms. Her tears fell like the rain, soaking through his shirt and touching his skin, his own eyes prickling with heat. He held her close for a long time, his breath coming in short gasps as he closed his eyes tightly, drinking in her presence. She trembled against him, her voice whispering his name over and over.

"I'm here," he reassured her, his lips brushing lightly against her forehead. "I'm here, Jacintha. You are quite safe."

When she looked up at him, Henry could not help but brush his lips against hers, only for her to press herself up and deepen their kiss, one arm going around his neck as she clung to him. He could not take it all in, his emotions swinging wildly from relief to happiness to fierce anger over what Lord Slate had done.

"Jacintha," he whispered, as he broke their kiss. Cradling her face in his hands, he looked down into her eyes, relieved to see that she was no longer crying. "I would have gone to the ends of the earth to find you."

She smiled tremulously, her eyes half closed as he brushed his fingers lightly down her cheeks. "I could only think of you," she whispered, leaning forward to rest her head against his chest. "You came for me."

"I will never leave your side again," Henry promised, holding her tightly for another moment before stepping back from her. "We must go up to the deck. My uncle is waiting there."

Jacintha shuddered violently. "Lord Slate?"

Henry frowned, his jaw clenching. "I will ensure that he is gone from the ship before we ascend, Jacintha, I promise you. You will never have to lay eyes on that man again."

She looked up at him again, her eyes trusting. "Thank you, Henry."

He smiled softly, more than relieved that he had her safely with him once more. "Come, then. Let us return you to your father and sister."

CHAPTER TWENTY-TWO

*J*acintha smiled and tried not to cry as Harmonia threw her arms around her, having clearly been in a state of panic over what had become of her sister.

"I am quite all right," Jacintha whispered, as Harmonia sobbed quietly. "Henry found me."

Harmonia wiped her eyes and shook her head, releasing her. "I was so afraid."

"What about Papa?" Jacintha asked, urgently. "Does he know?"

"No, but he must," Henry interrupted, putting one hand on her arm. "Come and sit down, Jacintha. Harmonia, might you go and ask your father to join us? It is best he hear all of this."

Jacintha looked back at Henry as he continued to reel off orders to the two maids who had joined them. A tea tray was sent for, a warm cloak and a fire to be stoked in the drawing room. Given that Jacintha and Harmonia's maids were the only two staff in the house – apart from her father's manservant – Jacintha appreciated that they were so willing to do as they were asked.

"Where are the rest of the staff?" Henry's uncle, asked, as Henry led Jacintha into the drawing room.

"Gone," Henry muttered, sitting down next to Jacintha. "They clearly knew of what Lord Slate was doing and have either left his house in case they were implicated – or because they knew he did not intend to return."

Roderick Larchmont shook his head, his eyebrows furrowed. "No matter. We have enough evidence on Slate regardless of their testimony."

"What is going to happen to him?" Jacintha asked, her fingers tightening in her lap as she twined them together. "To Lord Slate, I mean?"

Henry grunted. "That will be for the judge to decide. He will lose everything, however, I have no doubt, after what he did to you. Transportation, most likely."

"Death is not for noblemen," Uncle Larchmont murmured. "Then again, it depends if the rest of them are willing to talk about Lord Slate's involvement in order to save their own hides. I would guess that they will."

Jacintha made to ask whether or not all the smugglers had been taken to the local jail, only for her father to enter the room in a state of worry and confusion. Jacintha was wrapped in his embrace for a good minute or so and it took some time to calm him down long enough to explain exactly what had occurred.

Thankfully, a snifter of brandy helped the Duke to settle, although his face remained grave as Henry explained all that had occurred.

"But I thought Lord Slate to be such an amiable man," the Duke protested, his eyes widening as he looked over at Jacintha. "Did he not treat you well?"

Jacintha tried to smile, grateful that Harmonia was pouring the tea. "He did whilst we were in London, Papa, but not here."

Her father's eyes dimmed. "I should never have come here. I knew I should have returned home. I am certain I would not have become ill at home."

Harmonia took her father's hand, her expression gentle. "None of us had any expectation that Lord Slate would behave in such a way, Papa. This is not your doing."

"No, indeed," Henry repeated, firmly. "You must not blame yourself, Your Grace. None of you should take on any unfair responsibility."

"But to take you out to the ship, to take you to another land where I would never see you again!" the Duke exclaimed, his eyes on Jacintha. "I cannot bear the thought of it! And I thought he was nothing more than a gentleman – a gentleman who would set you up for the rest of your days."

"I am quite well now, Papa," Jacintha replied, even though she still felt rather weak from all that had occurred. "Henry was the one to find me and brought me back here. I am grateful to him for all that he did, as well as to you, Mr. Larchmont. Without you, I might never have returned to my family."

Henry put his hand on hers, ignoring the lack of propriety that this action brought. "You are stronger than I ever knew," he said softly, as Jacintha turned to look into his eyes, feeling warmth spill into her heart. "I cannot tell you how relieved I was to find you on board, hiding from that despicable man."

Jacintha's throat closed up, the words she wanted to say dying on her tongue. She wanted to tell him just how much she had thought of him, how the memory of him had sustained her when she had lost almost all hope. When he had first called her name, she had thought herself dreaming, lost in a haze of sorrow and fear – but when she had realized that it truly was Henry, her limbs had burst to life and she had scrambled to her feet, desperate to run to him for safety. The sight of him standing there, looking as terrified and as desolate as she felt had spoken to her heart. He had been lost without her, just as she had been without him.

To be in his arms again had been the most wonderful moment of her life.

"I owe you a great debt of gratitude," the Duke said, firmly, getting up to shake Henry's hand, followed by Roderick Larchmont's. "You have given me my daughter back."

Jacintha smiled as her father took her hand again, dismayed to see his expression growing sorrowful. "I thought Lord Slate was an excellent match," he muttered, as he went back to take his seat. "How could I have made such a poor judgment of his character?"

"Because he hid it well," Jacintha replied, softly. "Even I was taken in, Papa. I believed he held some affection for me, but once I came here, I discovered that he saw me as nothing more than a requirement. He thought he needed a wife in order to gain more respectability – as well as producing the heir," she continued, with a slight blush to her cheeks, "and that, since he had chosen me, he intended to fulfill his intentions."

Henry shook his head, his jaw set and fire burning in his gaze. "The man is a scoundrel and a rogue."

"He cared nothing for me," Jacintha murmured, her heart growing painful with the memory of what he had said to her so fiercely. "He had put in so much effort with me that he did not want to return to London in order to choose another. Besides, I found the passageway, which I was not meant to."

"The passageway?" Mr. Larchmont murmured, his eyebrows lifting just a little. "Where is that, if you please?"

"In the library," Jacintha replied, frowning as she tried to recall exactly. "There is a small portrait of a lady which, I believe, I bumped and, somehow, it opened the door to the passageway."

Mr. Larchmont got to his feet, clearing his throat. "I should find it, to ensure that we have all of our evidence written up," he said, with a slight incline of his head. "Do excuse me."

Jacintha saw her father look up at Roderick Larchmont for a moment, a slightly confused expression on his face. Clearly, there was a lot to take in and Jacintha could not blame her father for being rather befuddled by all that had gone on whilst he remained here in bed, recovering.

"Papa, I am sure Mr. Larchmont will not mind if you accompany him," she said softly, seeing Harmonia glance over at her in surprise. "Go and see the passageway and ask as many questions as you need. I shall be quite well here, I assure you."

Mr. Larchmont indicated his agreement at once and, after ensuring that Jacintha would, in fact, be quite all right, the Duke rose and followed after him, already asking about how Lord Slate had taken Jacintha out to the boat.

Jacintha looked over at Harmonia, who was studying Henry with a careful eye, a small smile on her face.

"I think I shall get some more tea," she murmured, her cheeks a light pink. "I shall only be a few minutes."

"Thank you, Harmonia," Jacintha replied, leaning back in her seat as a great tiredness swept through her. "You are very kind."

. . .

Silence swept over Jacintha and Henry as Harmonia's footsteps died away. Jacintha looked up at him, aware of his presence beside her. His eyes were fixed on hers, as though fastened there, and Jacintha found she could not look away. Her heart was filled with him, the regret she had once felt at turning away from him in order to choose Lord Slate dying away steadily.

"Jacintha," Henry began, hoarsely, taking a hold of her hand again. "I am glad to see you so restored to your family. Are you feeling any better?"

"Stronger, yes," she replied, despite the exhaustion flowing steadily through her. "Although I confess I am rather tired."

"How much you have endured," he murmured softly, his fingers running over the back of her hand. "And yet you are as serene as I have ever seen you."

She laughed then, her expression soft. "That is only because you cannot see my very soul tremble."

He did not laugh, his eyes grave. "I should have made more of an effort to speak to you," he said, his eyes lowering for a moment. "When Lord Slate turned myself and my uncle away at the door, I should have demanded to see you. Then none of this might have happened. I would have kept you safe over charging him for smuggling."

Wanting to relieve his anxiety, Jacintha leaned forward and ran her hand lightly down his cheek, her breath hitching as he looked up, intently, into her eyes. "Henry, you saved me. Forget what might have been or what could have happened, you rescued me from Lord Slate and from a life that would have been nothing more than misery and torment. I cannot tell you how grateful I am to you."

She saw him swallow, his eyes drawing her ever closer.

"I have never forgotten that moment in the garden," he whispered, one hand wrapping lightly around her waist. "I lost my way for a time, I forgot about who I was supposed to be, but I assure you that I will never turn that way again."

Aware of what he was saying, aware of what he was offering, Jacintha could not help but respond. Leaning forward, she touched her mouth to his, feeling her body ignite as she did so. Their kiss was long, slow and sweet, filled with promises and healing.

"I have never forgotten that moment either," she whispered, as he rested his forehead gently against her own. "I have always wondered what would have become of us should we not have been interrupted. For a long time, I convinced myself that marriage based on nothing more than convenience and practicality was what I wanted – but I know now that it is not the case. I want love, Henry. I want to be with the man I love, who loves me as much in return."

"I can give you that," he promised, his voice hoarse. "Jacintha, will you truly have me? Will you be my wife?"

Her heart filled with such happiness that she thought it might burst from her chest. "I will, Henry. Of course I will."

EPILOGUE

*H*enry paced up and down the room, running one hand through his hair as he waited in a state of anxiety for the doctor to leave his wife's room.

Jacintha had been pale and tired for weeks and, after some convincing, she had permitted him to send for the doctor. Terrified that she was ill, Henry tried not to allow his worry to cloud his mind, desperately waiting for the door to open so that he might be permitted.

After a few more minutes, the door opened and the doctor stepped out, a small smile on his face.

"Is she quite well?"

"Lots of rest," the doctor replied, patting Henry on the shoulder. "She needs to eat well and sleep any time she is tired. Ginger should help the sickness."

"Sickness?" Henry repeated, his eyes widening as he looked from the doctor into Jacintha's room. "She has been sick?"

"It will pass," the doctor replied, with a slight chuckle. "On you go then, Lord Musgrove. And do send for me again if it requires it."

More confused than ever, Henry rushed into the room, forgetting to thank the doctor entirely, and made his way over to Jacintha's side.

Much to his horror, there were tears trickling down her cheeks. "Oh, Jacintha," he whispered, sinking down on to the edge of the bed and taking her hand. "Whatever is the matter?" He could not understand why his wife was crying and the doctor smiling. If she was ill, then why had the man appeared so happy?

"Oh, Henry," Jacintha replied, her eyes turning towards him. "I cannot believe it."

"What?" he breathed, his stomach dropping like a stone. "What did the doctor say?"

"I should have noticed it myself, but with all the renovations we have been undertaking, I quite lost track," she continued, as though she had not heard him. "It should only be six months or so now."

Henry shook his head. "Six months?" he repeated, frowning heavily. "Jacintha, will you please tell me what is the matter?"

Much to his astonishment, Jacintha laughed and sat up a little straighter, her eyes bright. "Oh, Henry," she replied, softly, putting one gentle hand against his cheek. "Have you not worked it out yet? You are to be a father very soon."

Time stopped. He could not breathe. Could not think. Could not even form any words to express what he felt.

She laughed again, leaning forward to hug him tightly for a moment. "You look quite astonished, my love."

"With child?" Henry whispered, relief washing all through him. "You are with child? That is why you..."

"Why I have been so tired and weak, yes," Jacintha answered, her eyes gentle. "I was so worried, Henry, but the doctor reassured me that it was all quite normal and nothing to be worried about."

Henry felt like crying and laughing all at once, such was his astonishment and relief. He held Jacintha close for a long moment, letting out a few long, slow breaths in order to try and bring himself back to a place of composure.

"You are happy, are you not?" Jacintha asked, as he released her. "You are happy we are to have a child, yes?"

"Of course I am," Henry reassured her, with a glad smile. "A little taken aback but truly, I am delighted."

"I am very glad to hear it," Jacintha replied, softly. "Just think, Henry, a baby of our own! And we only married a few months."

Henry felt sheer joy bubble up in his chest, his eyes bright with happiness. "And here I was thinking that life could never get any happier than we are now," he replied, leaning forward to press a gentle kiss to her cheek. "Do you think your sisters will be glad to hear of it?"

Jacintha laughed again, her smile warm. "They will be delighted. Of course, I shall have to have them visit for I do not know what this state is to be like! Nor do I know much at all about babies..." Her smile began to fade, a worried look appearing on her face.

Now it was Henry's turn to laugh. "Do not worry, my love. You did not know anything about becoming a wife, but see how well you have mastered it? You shall be just as wonderful a mother as you are a wife, and I know that our child will be showered with love."

Her anxiety faded at once. "Thank you, Henry. You always know how to put me at ease."

"Although you will not be able to invite Harmonia," Henry joked, with a slight shake of his head. "She is the only sister remaining to find a husband, and we cannot impede her search."

Jacintha's smile was warm as she wrapped her arms around his neck and pulled him closer. "You are quite right. Harmonia needs to find a man who loves her and not settle for practicality."

Henry chuckled. "Just as you did?" he teased, only for her to cut off his words with a sound kiss.

"Yes, just as I did," she whispered against his mouth. "Ever since that day in the gardens, all those years ago."

Continue on now in the series with Harmonia's story, In the Arms of an Earl A sneak peek is just a few pages ahead!

Enjoying this book? Get the series with The Duke's Daughters Boxset.

MY DEAR READER

Thank you for reading and supporting my books! I hope this story brought you some escape from the real world into the always captivating Regency world. A good story, especially one with a happy ending, just brightens your day and makes you feel good! If you enjoyed the book, would you leave a review on Amazon? Reviews are always appreciated.

Below is a complete list of all my books! Why not click and see if one of them can keep you entertained for a few hours?

The Duke's Daughters Series
The Duke's Daughters: A Sweet Regency Romance Boxset
A Rogue for a Lady
My Restless Earl
Rescued by an Earl
In the Arms of an Earl
The Reluctant Marquess (Prequel)

A Smithfield Market Regency Romance
The Smithfield Market Romances: A Sweet Regency
Romance Boxset
The Rogue's Flower
Saved by the Scoundrel
Mending the Duke
The Baron's Malady

The Returned Lords of Grosvenor Square
The Returned Lords of Grosvenor Square: A Regency
Romance Boxset
The Waiting Bride
The Long Return
The Duke's Saving Grace
A New Home for the Duke

The Spinsters Guild
The Spinsters Guild: A Sweet Regency Romance Boxset
A New Beginning
The Disgraced Bride
A Gentleman's Revenge
A Foolish Wager
A Lord Undone

Convenient Arrangements
Convenient Arrangements: A Regency Romance
Collection
A Broken Betrothal
In Search of Love
Wed in Disgrace
Betrayal and Lies
A Past to Forget
Engaged to a Friend

Landon House
Landon House: A Regency Romance Boxset
Mistaken for a Rake
A Selfish Heart
A Love Unbroken
A Christmas Match
A Most Suitable Bride

An Expectation of Love

Second Chance Regency Romance
Second Chance Regency Romance Boxset
Loving the Scarred Soldier
Second Chance for Love
A Family of her Own
A Spinster No More

Soldiers and Sweethearts
To Trust a Viscount
Whispers of the Heart
Dare to Love a Marquess
Healing the Earl
A Lady's Brave Heart

Ladies on their Own: Governesses and Companions
Ladies on their Own Boxset
More Than a Companion
The Hidden Governess
The Companion and the Earl
More than a Governess
Protected by the Companion

Lost Fortunes, Found Love
A Viscount's Stolen Fortune
For Richer, For Poorer
Her Heart's Choice
A Dreadful Secret
Their Forgotten Love
His Convenient Match

Only for Love

The Heart of a Gentleman
A Lord or a Liar
The Earl's Unspoken Love

Christmas Stories
Love and Christmas Wishes: Three Regency Romance
Novellas
A Family for Christmas
Mistletoe Magic: A Regency Romance
Heart, Homes & Holidays: A Sweet Romance Anthology

Happy Reading!
All my love,
Rose

A SNEAK PEEK OF IN THE ARMS OF AN EARL

CHAPTER ONE

"*A*melia!"

Harmonia practically flew across the room, holding her sister in a tight embrace.

"It is so good to see you," she murmured, her heart squeezing with both happiness and sorrow. "I have missed you so very much."

Harmonia stepped back and wiped away a tear, her smile wobbling just a little. It had been almost a year since she had seen any of her sisters and she had found it a rather lonely one. Having been used to a home that was busy with her other three sisters and her father, it had been quite a shock to be all alone. Her father, the Duke of Westbrook, had been much recovered since his last bout of illness late last summer. Of course, she had his company but it had not been the same as the company of her sisters.

"I have missed you too," Amelia replied, with a soft smile. "Life has changed so much for me over these last years that I feel as though I need to get to know you all over again!"

"And now you have the opportunity," Harmonia replied

at once, leading her eldest sister over to where a tea tray sat waiting. "Are you quite sure your children will fare well without you?"

Amelia laughed and shook her head. "I am quite sure they will do very well," she replied, with a quick smile. "After all, Grace and Henry will very much enjoy the company of their cousins."

Harmonia sighed heavily, her smile fading. "I do miss the others." Both Jessica and Jacintha had married and now had children of their own, with Jacintha only just out of her confinement. Jessica had gone to visit Jacintha, as had Amelia, although Harmonia had been unable to do so since her father needed her at home. She still had not met Jacintha's little boy, but Harmonia comforted herself with the fact that she would be able to go and visit the family after the Season was over.

Amelia had only just come from Jacintha's home and, having left her children in the care of her two sisters, had chosen to come to London in order to chaperone Harmonia during the London Season, knowing that she would require some assistance. Harmonia and Amelia had always been very close, and Harmonia was grateful for her sister's kindness, especially when she knew that Amelia would miss both her children and her husband, Lord Northfell.

"I know you miss them but in time, we shall all be together again," Amelia said, softly. "Now it is the time for you to find your own happiness, Harmonia. I can tell that you have been lonely over this last year and I am sorry for it. Had I known, I would have come to stay with you and Papa."

Harmonia gave her sister a small smile, aware that she was unable to hide anything from her. "It has just taken a little time to become used to my new situation," she said, honestly. "Papa has been in good spirits and I *am* glad that he has been able to return to London."

Amelia accepted the cup of tea from Harmonia and sat back in her chair. "I know he is hoping to have you wed very soon."

Harmonia lifted her eyebrows in surprise. "You saw him?"

"He was waiting for me as I came into the house," Amelia replied, with a quick smile. "He appeared rather tired though, so we did not talk for long."

Harmonia nodded slowly. "We only arrived in London a few days ago and the travelling does make him rather weary." She bit her lip, remembering what her father had said to her. "Papa is quite insistent that I find a suitor this Season."

"Indeed," Amelia agreed. "I had hoped he would be a little more relaxed now that three of his daughters are wed, but this does not seem to be the case."

Sighing, Harmonia shook her head. "He was very much that way with Jacintha, but I wonder if my being alone with him in the house has made him realize his fears all over again."

"That he will pass away and our futures will be in jeopardy," Amelia murmured, thoughtfully. "But he need not worry in that regard. He *must* know that we would take care of you should that happen – not that I think it will, of course."

Harmonia shook her head, taking a long sip of her tea. "And cousin Luke is in town."

Amelia's mouth fell open for a moment, her eyes widening. "Harmonia, he is not still pursuing you?"

"I have received many letters from him over the course of the last year," Harmonia replied, frankly. "He reminds me that he is, in fact, a distant cousin and not a close relative, as though that might encourage me to consider his suit."

"I hope you are not allowing thoughts of Luke to pervade your mind," Amelia replied at once, putting her cup and saucer down on the table. "You told me you were set against him."

"I thought I was," Harmonia replied, quietly. "I mean, I still think that he is not the best prospect I could hope for but what if he is the *only* prospect?" Her words tumbled from her mouth, her deepest fears being revealed to her older sister all at once. "I am the youngest of four daughters, my dowry less than the rest of you and rather shy and quiet." Feeling tears pricking at her eyes, she leaned forward to pour herself some more tea, hoping that her sister would not see how deeply upset she was. "I have never had my dance card completely filled at any ball we have ever attended, and I find myself something of a wallflower at such events. I have never been able to continue a conversation with the ease that you do, nor caught the eye of a gentleman simply by smiling at him, as Jessica did. I do not have Jacintha's confidence nor your calm character. I am shy and retiring and far too quiet. What if Luke is the only prospect I shall ever have?"

There was silence for a long time. Amelia, her hands folded in her lap, studied Harmonia for a few moments before letting out one long breath, a sad smile on her face.

"My very dear Harmonia, do you truly see yourself in such a way?"

Harmonia, who had been fighting tears, tried to look steadily at her sister. "I don't know what you mean."

"You are so lacking in confidence that you do not see yourself as others do," Amelia replied, still smiling at her.

"You are kind and sweet and gentle, with a heart so filled with compassion and tenderness that I have often envied you. You may be quiet or feel as though you lack the ability to converse easily with others but that is not what matters, Harmonia. A character such as yours will shine through regardless of what is going on around you. A smile from you and a gentleman will be quite lost. You are beautiful, Harmonia, truly. This Season will be your time to shine forth – and a gentleman willing to pursue your heart is a gentleman who will be worthy of you. Have no fear as to your prospects, dear sister. Luke is not the gentleman for you, as you and I have discussed so many times. He does not care about your heart. He only cares about the connection he will have with the family. He wants to have that closeness to our father, for whatever reason."

Harmonia swallowed the lump in her throat and tried to smile. "You are very kind, Amelia."

"Every word I say is true," Amelia promised, a gentle smile on her face. "Now, you must forget Luke entirely and, even if he does attend the same events as we do, we will not give him too much attention. He will have to understand that you are not to be his, no matter how much he pursues you."

Harmonia nodded slowly, trying to take in all that Amelia had said. The truth was that she had never seen herself as anything other than a quiet mouse, hiding behind the rest of her sisters as though afraid of what would come to face her when it was her turn to enter society. Now, however, she was to have no choice. Amelia would be her support, her guide. She did not, at least, have to face this new world alone.

"Now, I think we must get you out of the house and into town," Amelia said with a smile, getting to her feet and stepping out towards the door. "You will not lose your melancholy simply by sitting here and trying to gain reassurance from my words. We are to go to the shops!"

"The shops?" Harmonia echoed, almost tripping over her own feet as she hurried after Amelia. "Whatever for?"

"For gowns, of course," Amelia replied, her eyes dancing. "We have Lord Gaynes ball tomorrow evening and I insist that you have a new gown."

"I do not need a new gown," Harmonia replied, following Amelia out into the hallway. "All of my gowns from last year are still quite respectable."

Amelia turned around and took Harmonia's hand, coming to a complete stop. "No, Harmonia, you are to have a few new gowns, I insist upon it. Some, of course, will take some time to create but there should be something that will only need a few alternations for tomorrow evening. When it was my turn to enter society, that is what I had and so the same shall be given to you. It is only fair. Besides, I think I will be able to help you find the most beautiful of gowns, ones that will ensure you are simply unable to fade into the background, as you put it."

Harmonia hesitated for a moment before she relented. If she was to have any prospects other than Luke, then she was going to have to do her best to meet new acquaintances. She felt as though she was being selfish in having new gowns simply for herself, but she knew that Amelia would not relent. It was best just to do as her eldest sister thought best.

"Excellent," Amelia exclaimed, turning on her heel and practically marching towards the staircase that would lead to the front door. "What you're wearing is quite respectable, although you will need a bonnet and possibly your shawl if there is still that cool breeze. We will not require a maid since I am an old married woman now and, therefore, quite respectable enough to chaperone you."

Harmonia, now feeling a great deal more cheerful, tied her bonnet ribbons and smiled at her sister. "Thank you, Amelia. I am feeling better already."

Amelia smiled, looped her arm through Harmonia's and left the house. "And it is only going to get better from here on out, I promise you," she said before the two sisters made their way into town.

CHAPTER TWO

"*A*re you quite ready?"

Harmonia drew in a deep breath before giving Amelia a bright smile. "Yes, I think so."

"Good," Amelia replied, as the carriage drew up to Lord Gaynes home. It was a large, ornate building with its own large gardens both front and back. The carriage rolled through the gates and made its way up to the house, leaving Harmonia feeling more and more nervous.

"Now, if Luke is here, as you expect him to be, then I insist that you allow me to try and take his attention away from you for a time," Amelia began, as they joined the long line of carriages letting people down one at a time in front of the house. "You told me you would not think of him in a serious manner and I must insist that you continue to think of him in that way."

Harmonia tried to nod, her stomach roiling with a sudden nausea.

"I do know, however, that cousin Luke can be a very insistent man, so it may prove a little more difficult than I am suggesting," Amelia continued, with a wry smile. "Do ensure that you have time away from him, time to be introduced to new acquaintances for example. You are never going to find a suitable match if you do not get yourself away from Luke, Harmonia. Do you understand?"

"Yes, of course," Harmonia said, quickly. "Goodness, I did not expect to feel this nervous."

Amelia laughed softly, her eyes growing a little distant. "It feels very different when it is you who is the focus," she said, quietly. "With all your sisters married, the *ton* will know that it is you who is now to find a husband. That fact cannot be hidden."

Feeling as though every eye was to be on her the moment she stepped from the carriage, Harmonia drew in long, deep breaths in an effort to calm her nerves. Amelia murmured a few soothing words and, once they had descended from the carriage, took her arm and began to climb the few short steps that led to the front of the house.

"You need not look so worried, Harmonia," Amelia chided gently, as they came to the front door. "Try to smile, my dear sister. Wipe that anxiety from your face."

With an effort, Harmonia lifted her chin and smiled gently as she stepped inside, nodding to a few people she recognized. Once they had greeted and thanked the hosts, Harmonia and Amelia walked a little further into the house before coming to the ballroom.

The orchestra was already playing, and the dancing in full swing. Harmonia felt her smile stretch as she watched the spinning couples, her anxiety slowly beginning to fade. This was what she had been missing during her year at home – company, dancing, conversation and laughter. There was plenty of that here, however. She just needed to let herself relax and enjoy the evening. It was not as though she were expected to find a husband this very evening!

"Lady Harmonia? Lady Harmonia!"

Jerking in surprise, Harmonia felt Amelia clutch at her arm, giving her a gentle tug to her left but, before she could move, none other than Luke appeared in front of them both, a wide smile on his face.

"Lady Harmonia, how good to see you," he said, with a deep bow. "I have been waiting for your arrival and sighted you almost the moment you stepped inside."

Before Harmonia could reply, Amelia cleared her throat loudly, drawing Luke's attention. He colored at once, aware of his rudeness, and bowed quickly before greeting her.

"I did not see you there, Lady Amelia. I do apologize. And your father? Is he here?"

"No, he is not," Amelia answered, before Harmonia could say a word. "He is tired and remained at home. *I* am Harmonia's chaperone."

Luke did not seem to notice her, his attention entirely fixed on Harmonia. "And do you have your dance card? I simply must put my name on it. How glad I am that I found you the moment you stepped into the ballroom. I could not have allowed the evening to go by without ensuring I had at least one dance with you. Mayhap the waltz would be suitable?"

Harmonia's mouth went dry, glancing towards Amelia for help. Luke was always so sure of himself, so certain of what he wanted. Despite Harmonia's attempts at pushing him away, he had never taken her refusal to be a definitive answer. Even now, he was suggesting that they waltz together in the hope that he might somehow endear her further towards him.

"Come now, Lord Darnsley," Amelia admonished, using his formal title and, with a wave of her hand, blowing his suggestion away. "The waltz simply will *not* do, not for someone who is family to us. We do not want to suggest that there is anything more than familial friendship between yourself and Harmonia."

Luke cleared his throat, his eyebrows furrowing. "Lady Amelia, I had hoped –"

"*Do* hurry, Luke, please," Amelia interrupted, still looking quite disinterested. "I must introduce Harmonia to a few new acquaintances."

Harmonia gave him a quick smile as he muttered darkly under his breath before signing her dance card. Much to her surprise, he *did* write his name under one of the waltzes, despite Amelia's express request that he did not. His doggedness had come to the fore once again.

As Luke scribbled his name, Harmonia was caught by a movement to her left and, on looking over, saw a gentleman regarding her. He had the bluest eyes she had ever seen and, when she saw him watching, he simply smiled and did not look away. Her heart quickened, her breath hitching as he turned away from her, leaving her to wonder who he might be and why he had been watching her. She tried to recall whether or not she had seen him before, giving herself a slight shake as Luke dropped her dance card.

"I look forward to our dance, Harmonia," Luke murmured, as he gave her a quick bow. "Thank you."

Realizing that she had not yet uttered a single word to him, Harmonia tried to smile and thank him, her voice a little hoarse.

"Regardless of what Amelia believes, you know what my intentions are, Harmonia," Luke continued, so softly that Harmonia had to strain to hear him. "Do not forget that."

He turned around and walked away into the crowd, leaving her to stare after him. Apparently, she had not convinced him about her lack of regard, even though it had been made clear to him multiple times. Deep in her heart, she had hoped that he might come to accept how she felt, that he might even be caught by another young lady's attentions, but it appeared not to be the case.

"What did he say to you?" Amelia murmured, as they began to walk through the guests once more. "And what dances did he put himself down for?"

Harmonia shook her head, lifting her dance card. "The quadrille and the waltz."

Amelia stopped dead, her face a mixture of frustration and anger. "I specifically said –"

"He is used to getting what he wants," Harmonia reminded her, with a slight shrug. "I cannot refuse him."

Amelia shook her head, her face a little red. "You could always be in the retiring room when it is time for the waltz," she muttered, before continuing to walk to the side of the ballroom. "Come now, we need to greet a few more acquaintances."

Harmonia smiled and nodded to a few more of her friends, before being greeted by a gentleman she did not recognize. He seemed to know Amelia and Lord Northfell. That led to even more introductions to other ladies and gentlemen and, very soon, Harmonia had her dance card all but filled. It brought her a great deal of happiness to know that she was wanted and desired by those in the room, that her company was now sought after. She did not feel like the wallflower she usually was at such things as this, grateful for Amelia's guidance and help.

Listening politely to one gentleman talking about his recent purchase of a pair of greys, Harmonia suddenly caught sight of the blue-eyed gentlemen from only a few minutes before. He was now talking to a young lady, standing just behind Amelia. She could not help but study him for a moment, taking in his strong features and broad shoulders. He was impeccably dressed, with not so much as a hair out of place and, for whatever reason, Harmonia felt drawn to him.

Which was quite ridiculous, given that she did not so much as know his name. As she gave herself a stern talking to, the gentleman looked up and caught her gaze, only for Harmonia to drag hers immediately away from him and back to the gentlemen who had been speaking to her about his stables. A flush of embarrassment crept up into her cheeks, almost feeling the blue-eyed gentleman's gaze remaining on her – although she dared not look back at him. It was almost a relief when Lord Donaghy came to claim her for his dance for that meant she was no longer in close proximity to the mysterious gentlemen. At least while dancing, she would no longer feel confused and distracted by him. She needed to focus on making sure each step was done correctly.

Lord Donaghy was a polite, genteel young man with a sparkling wit and sharp eyes. He complimented her on her dancing, smiled at her response and made a joke about one of the fop's choice of cravat which made Harmonia laugh. He was, all in all, a very nice young man although there was no spark of interest in Harmonia's heart.

When the dance came to a close, Lord Donaghy led her back towards Amelia, still chatting amicably. Harmonia was enjoying the conversation, but her response died on her lips as she saw her sister talking with a small group of gentlemen and ladies, which included the blue-eyed gentleman from before.

Her heart began to hammer wildly in her chest as she

drew near, seeing the gentleman look over at her, his smile widening as he took her in.

"Ah, Harmonia," her sister exclaimed, a smile on her face. "I was just making some new acquaintances although, I confess, that I have not quite got to know everyone's name just yet! Of course, you know Lady Sophia Winterthorn."

"Yes, yes of course," Harmonia replied, a little breathlessly. "This is Lord Donaghy, to those of you who might not know him."

Lord Donaghy gave a short bow, the conversation beginning to flow again – and yet Harmonia could not look anywhere but the blue-eyed gentleman.

"I confess that I do not yet know your name," the blue-eyed gentleman asked her, seemingly ignorant of everyone else around him.

His voice was deep and rich, his expression warm as he drew near her. Harmonia drew in a sharp breath, her skin tingling all over as he smiled at her.

"This is precisely why I have come to London, sir," she replied, quickly, hoping that she was not speaking too quickly nor appearing too eager. "My acquaintances are in much smaller number in the country, mostly because there is a severe lack of society particularly during the winter."

She was babbling now. She knew it and her cheeks warmed immediately.

"I quite understand," he said with a smile, his gaze still fixed on her own. "I suppose we must give up convention and introduce ourselves to one another without your sister or another being involved."

Harmonia felt her smile spread across her face, pleasure spinning through her. "Indeed, I think we must. I am –"

"Ah, there you are!"

A loud, brash voice interrupted her and, looking behind

her, Harmonia saw none other than Luke striding towards her.

"Come now, it is our dance and I will not lose this opportunity," Luke said, coming to stand beside her, her gaze on the gentleman she had been talking to. "Nor will I give you up to another."

Harmonia, mortified by Luke's arrogant speech, turned towards him and gave him a tight smile. "Yes, of course," she said at once, suddenly desperate to get Luke as far away from the gentlemen as she could. "Do excuse me, sir," she murmured, giving the gentleman one last look, trying to hide her frustration that she still did not know his name.

"But of course," he replied, with an easy smile. "I will not keep you. Good evening."

Harmonia did not have time to reply, having been quickly hurried away by Luke. She did not enjoy the dance, despite Luke's clear delight at having her all to himself. She found him frustrating, irritating and much too full of himself. He did not take her refusal of his intentions to marry her seriously, seemingly believing that if he continued to pursue her enough, she would simply agree. Was she truly that weak? Did he see her as this small, easily intimidated, eventually willing to do what he asked if he pressured her enough?

The evening began to lose some of its sparkle, her heart sinking into her toes as Luke twirled her around the floor and, suddenly, all she wanted was to return home.

CHAPTER THREE

"*D*id you enjoy the ball last evening?"

Harmonia threw a sidelong glance over towards Amelia as they walked through the park, wondering how much to give away. "I *was* enjoying myself until Luke..."

Amelia sighed as Harmonia struggled to find the words to explain his behavior last night.

"Luke acted rather possessive, did he not?"

"Yes, that is it precisely," Harmonia agreed, with a small shake of her head. "He seems to think that I belong to him when, all the while, I have been doing all I can to dissuade him."

Amelia grimaced. "Maybe I should say something to him."

Harmonia shook her head. "I do not think he would so much as listen." Frowning, she paused in her walk and looked over at her sister. "You do not think he would go to Papa directly, do you? As I said, Papa is now quite eager for me to wed and I know he has a fondness for Luke."

Her sister did immediately answer, making Harmonia's worry rise even further.

"I do not know *what* Luke will do in order to get what he wants," Amelia replied, eventually. "But you should perhaps speak to Papa before Luke has the chance, just in case you are right to be as worried as you are. I can go with you, if you wish."

Harmonia nodded slowly, her stomach tightening. "I may take you up on that offer, Amelia. I am concerned that Luke is determined to have me as his wife – but I am equally determined to refuse him. I do not think that he expects me to be so stubborn, however. I think he believes that he can bend me to his will in time."

"Then you shall just have to make yourself more than clear over and over until he finally backs away," Amelia declared, now appearing a little cross over Luke's behavior. "Why that man has been intent on pursuing you, I shall never understand." Throwing a quick look over at Harmonia, Amelia tried to smile. "Not that you are not worth pursing, Harmonia, but not by a man who has been told repeatedly that you are not interested in furthering your acquaintance with him. He is as stubborn as a mule!" She tossed her head and began to walk again, muttering to herself.

Harmonia smiled to herself and continued to walk alongside her sister, her anxiety slowly fading away. She knew that Amelia would stick by her and was truly grateful for her company, especially when it came to matters of the heart. Amelia had been through a difficult time herself before she found Lord Northfell and she appreciated her determination to ensure that Harmonia was, in no way, to be tied to Luke.

"Might I ask, was your attention caught by anyone else

at the ball last evening?" Amelia asked, after a few minutes of silence. "You were introduced to a great many people, I know, but was there anyone in particular you might wish to know more about?"

Immediately, the image of the blue-eyed gentleman threw itself into Harmonia's mind and she felt her face blush with just the thought of him. Knowing that she could be entirely honest with Amelia, Harmonia told her about the man in question.

"I was actually wondering if you knew a certain gentleman's name," she began, as Amelia lifted one eyebrow in anticipation. "The only reason I am asking is because I was in the middle of conversation with him – a bit of a strange conversation since neither of us had been introduced – but we were about to give one another our names and titles when Luke came to take me for the next dance."

Amelia pursed her lips, thinking hard. "He was in the group with us?"

"Yes, he was," Harmonia replied, her heart quickening just a little as she thought of him. "He had the bluest eyes I have ever seen and very dark hair. He was tall, even taller than Luke, and yet gave all the appearances of gentleness. I know it was most improper to be talking in such an easy manner without being introduced, but there was no-one able to do so and I did very much want to talk to him."

Amelia laughed, looping her arm through her sister's. "You need not worry about that, Harmonia, certainly not for my sake. Convention has to be ignored sometimes, particularly at a ball! The man you are describing is, I think, the new Earl of Newford. He is only recently arrived in town, I think. I am quite sure we will see him again very soon at some ball or another." She gave Harmonia a sidelong glance, her eyes filled with interest. "Do you think you might like to know him better?"

"I do," Harmonia replied, honestly. "He seemed like a pleasant fellow and I do think I would like to know him a little more."

Harmonia likes "the blue-eyed gentleman"! Find out if they get together in the rest of the story, available in the Kindle store, In the Arms of an Earl

JOIN MY MAILING LIST

Sign up for my newsletter to stay up to date on new releases, contests, giveaways, freebies, and deals!

Free book with signup!

Monthly Facebook Giveaways! Books and Amazon gift cards!
Join me on Facebook: https://www. facebook.com/rosepearsonauthor

Website: www.RosePearsonAuthor.com

Follow me on Goodreads: Author Page

Printed in Dunstable, United Kingdom